DARK VACANCY

A LANCE BRODY NOVEL (BOOK 4)

MICHAEL ROBERTSON, JR.

DARK VACANCY

THE BOY KNEW HIS END WOULD COME.

He'd known for the past year, and he knew this truth the same way he knew certain other things—inexplicably. *A message from the stars*, he liked to say to himself and his family. No reason or logic or rationale. Just an understanding that he'd been given information in a way nobody else could comprehend. Well, not nobody.

There were others.

Few, indeed. But they were out there, all the same. Some had already fallen victim, some were perhaps past their prime, too old and too tired to be of much value to either side, but they all lived with their gifts. He wondered if they knew about each other, or if he was alone in the knowledge that others existed. If he'd been bestowed these facts to serve some further purpose, be part of a grander plan.

He wondered if the others had felt the moment the one had joined them. Because for the boy, in the moment he could only infer marked the birth of this new force among them, it was as if time had temporarily stopped. All hatred and evil and disgust had been erased and replaced with a great tidal wave of happiness that crashed to the ground and washed away all that was not pure.

It had felt like salvation. So that was what the boy decided to call the one—Salvation.

But the boy was not naïve enough to believe it was going to be over soon—this ongoing war between the light and the darkness. There would still be much suffering, much struggle and pain and confusion and anger and everything else that drained the human soul. There would be these things for Salvation, too. Maybe most of all. But if anybody was going to have the strength and determination to survive it all, it was that one.

The boy was only disappointed in the fact that he would not be around to see it.

Because the boy's end was here, and he knew, in the manner in which only he could know things, that Salvation's work would not come for several years. Long after the boy's body would be laid to rest in the earth.

He tried to focus on the memory of that moment when time had stopped and the wave of happiness had crashed, but he was failing.

The pain of the present was too much.

The other side knew that Salvation now walked among them. They wanted to find it before it was too late, wanted to use it for their own, help them accomplish their ultimate goal. The goal that the boy—and presumably the others like him—worked to stop. Whether directly or indirectly, consciously or subconsciously, they worked to keep the light shining into the darkness.

The darkness was here now. It'd found the boy and it wanted to know what he knew. It wanted to know what he didn't, as well. And that was the bigger problem.

The Reverend sat on the edge of one of the double beds in the small motel room and watched as the Surfer stood back from the boy tied to the chair and waited for further instructions. They'd been at this for nearly an hour, and the boy had proven to be much more resilient to both of their certain methods of persuasion than the Reverend had anticipated.

The boy was seventeen years old—nearly a man by legal standards—yet he possessed a mental fortitude and psychological strength well beyond his years. He'd built up several walls, layers of defense to keep them out. And that was what the Surfer, with the Reverend's help, had been working on for the past hour—tearing the walls down, brick by brick.

They were essentially destroying the boy's mind. Ripping apart his memories and shredding his intelligence until all that remained was fragmented and scattered tatters of who the boy had once been.

The Reverend didn't care about any of this. All he wanted was the golden egg hidden behind those walls. Information about this new and powerful presence he'd felt. And it wasn't just he who'd taken notice. Those he served had felt it as well, and they'd made his mission very clear.

Find it. Make it one for us. If it won't turn, kill it.

The task was proving much more difficult than the Reverend had imagined. The other side was doing well to protect this new force, shielding it from the prying eyes of the darkness until it was strong enough to fend for itself.

But they would find it. Not today, and maybe not for years to come, but they would succeed. And first, this boy would tell them what he knew.

The Reverend nodded once and the Surfer stepped forward, placing one large and tanned hand on the boy's slumped head. The boy's body jolted, jerking in one massive spasm as the Surfer tore free another couple bricks from the walls the boy had built in his mind. The boy's face was electric with pain, lips pressed tight and eyes squeezed shut. Tears leaking down his cheeks.

But he did not cry out.

In fact, he'd said nothing.

Not a word for the last hour.

From the rubble of the boy's mind, they'd managed to scrape out only a single word of the information he'd been protecting. For the moment, it was useless. Down the road, it might be enough. But there was more, and the Reverend wanted it.

The Surfer bore down, digging in deeper with his own gifts, and the boy's body went rigid against the chair. His eyes fluttered open, revealing only the whites. Drool slid from the boy's mouth, and just as the Reverend was about to intervene, stop the Surfer before he completely wiped the boy away without getting what they'd come for, the door to the motel room swung open hard and fast, slamming into the wall.

Which was odd, because the Reverend had made certain to lock the door before they'd started. After the lock, he had put up a barrier that drew its energy from the darkness, to further thwart any external forces that might try to interfere.

The Reverend jumped from the bed and the Surfer spun around, facing the doorway, letting the boy's body collapse onto itself in the chair.

The doorway was empty. Snow blew in on the howling wind, swirling its way down to salt the carpet.

The Reverend called out an angry, "Who's there?" and got no reply. He took a step forward, ready to look outside, but the Surfer stopped him with a hand on his shoulder, gently pulling him back.

The Reverend looked to him and asked, "What? What is it?"

The Surfer did not reply, but the Reverend watched as his partner's eyes squinted, seemingly locking onto something unseen to anyone else. Then his head slowly turned and followed it, as if something was moving across the motel room, sliding in among the shadows.

From behind them, suddenly the boy started to laugh. A slow, weak chuckle that gradually grew louder before it abruptly cut off.

When the Reverend turned around to face the boy, the boy's eyes were wide and alert once more, as if he'd used all his remaining strength for this one moment.

"He's ... here," the boy said, his voice barely above a whisper.

The Reverend looked to the Surfer, whose eyes were still locked onto something in the room with them, as if two predators were waiting to pounce on each other. Then he stepped closer to the boy and asked, "Who?"

The boy smiled. "Salvation."

And then the room exploded.

It had not been the best idea.

Lance Brody could admit that easily enough. When the man driving the box truck—his name was Neil, and he'd been traveling north to Scranton, Pennsylvania, to help his daughter move into a new apartment—had slowed the vehicle down and pulled to the side of the road a few yards shy of the interstate on-ramp, he'd given Lance a choice.

"Straight shot from here for me," Neil had said. He tapped the dirty plastic of the truck's dashboard. "Got just about enough gas to get to Scranton, so I won't be stopping anywhere else. You wanna ride, or do you want to call it quits here?" He nodded through the large windshield toward the small cluster of dirty and faded road signs by the on-ramp. "There's a town a few miles up the road. Been there once, years ago. Not much to look at, but it's there all the same. I'm sure you'll be able to..." He stopped himself, thought for a moment. "Well, I'm sure you'll be able to figure something out. Whatever it is you're after."

Lance looked through the windshield and down the lonely-looking road that stretched beyond. The sky was gray, and the grass and trees and asphalt looked cold and unkind. A gust of wind rushed from behind them and rattled the truck. And with it came the prickling at the back of Lance's skull.

He glanced to the beginning of the on-ramp. The gateway to another couple hours and over a hundred miles distance between him and Sugar Beach—between him and the Reverend and the Surfer. Despite what had happened there, what he'd seen and experienced on that night on the shore, Lance would not—*could* not—bring himself to accept that they were truly finished.

Going with Neil would be the better option. The choice that most people would have made.

But Lance Brody was not most people. And he was never truly alone.

The prickling at the base of his skull was one of the constant reminders of his omnipresent traveling companion, and also his obligation. His duty. His burden. His gifts.

He was supposed to get out here. And to the outside world, it was not the best idea. But to Lance, it was the one he would have to accept.

Acceptance. That was a theme he was all too familiar with, if not completely at ease with. Arguing for understanding did Lance little good. In fact, it often complicated things. Better to just roll with the punches and see where he ended up. Because for better or worse, he always landed exactly where he was supposed to. Even if he sometimes had to fight for it.

"I appreciate the ride and the offer, sir. But I'll get out here. You've been very kind to take me this far." Lance stuck out his hand and smiled at the man.

Neil sighed, shook his head. "Good luck, kid." Then, with the compassionate voice of the father in him coming to the surface, he shook Lance's hand and said, "Be careful out there, alright? I hate to say it, but it seems this day and age, there's more bad ones than good ones, you know?"

Lance didn't know if he believed this. He liked to think the world was still full of good, but the bad was just much better at making itself known.

"Yes, sir. I'll be careful. And thanks for being one of the good ones. I hope your daughter likes her new place. Drive safe."

And when Lance shouldered his backpack and made to grab the door handle, Neil quickly blurted, "I can pay you."

Lance stopped. Turned back toward the man. "I'm sorry?"

Neil rubbed at the back of his neck, looked out through the windshield and down the desolate road. "I mean ... it's just, I could use some help with moving her, you know? My daughter. I'm not as young as I used to be, and well, furniture is heavy. Even that cheap stuff from IKEA. Between you and me, her boyfriend's a wimp and probably couldn't carry his laptop down the stairs without breaking a sweat, forget about a sofa. I could pay you to help."

Lance smiled and wished he could explain more to the man. Help to set his mind at ease. This stranger cared about his well-being. *One of the good ones, for sure*, Lance thought.

"I'm sorry, sir. But I have to go. Thank you, again."

Without waiting for a response, Lance Brody opened the truck's door and stepped down onto the shoulder of the road. He stepped back and heard Neil shift into drive, and then the engine rumbled and the truck pulled slowly away, flashing its brake lights in a farewell salute before it climbed the on-ramp and left Lance standing alone on the side of the road in the middle of nowhere.

And then the snow had arrived.

Lance had started walking down the rural road, past the faded road signs and the interstate on-ramp and toward the town that Neil—and presumably one of the road signs, had they been more legible—had promised him would be a few miles away. He'd made it maybe a quarter mile before the already-gray sky had dimmed several shades darker, the air carrying crisp bites on the intensifying wind.

The storm arrived swiftly and without much preamble, the snow falling heavy and fast. In a matter of minutes, Lance's sneakers were trudging through an inch of the stuff. The hood of his sweatshirt was cinched as tightly around his face as he could get it, and he'd pulled his hands inside his sleeves and then buried them in the front pouch. The bare parts of his legs sticking out from his cargo shorts became speckled white. Melting snow began to trickle down his ankles and into his socks. The wind whipped around him in a frenzy, swirling snow and throwing it into his face. Lance squinted his eyes and said bad words under his breath, trying not to think about how warm the box truck's heater would be right about now, as Neil cruised along the interstate.

Lance kept walking.

What choice did he have? He'd seen no cars coming or going in either direction, and on both sides of the road there was nothing but fields and the distant tree line of heavy woods. No farms or houses. No shops or diners. Nothing. This was no-man's-land. A cut-through route from one side of civilization to another.

A great place to dump a body, he thought, surprising himself at his own morbid joke. But if anybody fully understood the evil that human beings were capable of, it was him.

He shivered at his own thoughts, and then another assault of wind whipped at the fabric of his hoodie. Tried to sneak underneath and grab his flesh with icy fangs. Lance pressed on, growing increasingly irritated as the wind continued to roar and the temperature continued to drop and the snow continued to pile up.

The road became completely white, making it impossible to tell where the asphalt ended and the shoulder began. Lance moved further to his left, imagining he was now walking directly down the center of the road, wanting the reassurance of hard ground beneath him as to not twist an ankle in some unseen dip or hill or hole in the earth along the shoulder. Ahead of him, he'd be able to see headlights easily enough to avoid oncoming traffic. Behind him, he hoped for the same—a sound of a growling engine or the splash of his shadow across the ground as warm lights grew brighter. If a car came from behind, he'd stick out his thumb and hope for a ride.

Because if nothing else, the prickling at the base of his skull back in the box truck had told Lance everything he needed to know—for now, that was. He was supposed to be walking this direction. Toward the town. And despite his near complete lack of understanding about how and why the Universe operated—especially when it came to his own abilities and inclinations—he had grown to trust it enough to believe he would make it to his destination.

Unless the Universe was as awful at predicting the weather as your average meteorologist, and this snowstorm had come as a surprise. If that was the case, he might die of hypothermia. But he supposed there were worse ways to go.

His mother had always loved snow. Fall was her favorite season—as it was his, too—but that didn't stop her from marveling at the beauty of a fresh blanket of snow. He'd found her many mornings standing on their small back patio after a night of snowfall, wearing her warm winter robe and her snow boots, a mug of tea steaming in her hand, held closely to her lips.

She'd stand motionless, save the occasional sips of tea, staring out at their backyard, taking in the wonder.

"I love the sound," she'd said to him once, when she'd caught him watching her from the opened patio sliding door.

"The sound?" he'd asked, lowering his own mug of coffee.

"The silence that comes with snow." She turned and smiled at him. "It helps mute everything that's not pure."

Pamela Brody said a lot of things that Lance wasn't sure he ever understood fully. Including her dying words to him: "*Go, Lance. It's only what's right. I love you.*"

And then she was gone. Her sacrifice complete. Leaving him to uphold his end of the terrible bargain.

A vibration on Lance's leg snapped him out of his memory and back to the bitter cold of the present. It pulsed a steady rhythm, paused, and then began to pulse again. He regrettably pulled one hand free from his hoodie's pouch, the cold air stinging his bared fingers, and then stuffed his hand into the pocket of his shorts, pulling out his cell phone.

The old flip phone's tiny blue screen weakly displayed her name.

Leah.

They'd not spoken since earlier that morning, which now felt like a very long time ago, as Lance had just agreed to take Neil up on his offer of a ride. Which had only been a short couple of hours since that fateful showdown on the beach with his foes. Looking around him now, as Lance found himself caught in the middle of a snowstorm, it seemed impossible that twenty-four hours ago he'd been walking the streets of Sugar Beach and enjoying an unseasonably warm day. It was as if he'd entered another world. Another time.

Droplets of snow peppered his phone's screen, blotting out her name. He wiped at them with the sleeve of his sweatshirt and flipped the phone open, pressing it hard to his ear to help cut out the sound of the wind.

"Hello?"

Nothing. A bit of dead air and the hiss of static.

"Hello? Leah?"

"Lance ... are you...?"

Lance stopped walking. Pressed the flat of his palm against his other ear. "Leah? Can you hear me?"

"Can't hear ... driving ... okay?"

Lance pulled the phone away from his ear and checked the reception bars. Found only the single tiny one still present. The one that basically said, *Screw you, we both know I'm worthless.* But to make matters worse, his battery was nearly dead.

He put the phone back to his ear and said, "Hey, I don't know if you can hear me or not, but I'm okay. My phone's about to die, but I want you to know I haven't forgotten what I said earlier. I promise I'll let you know as soon as—"

There were three quick beeps in his ear and then silence.

His phone had died.

Lance said another bad word under his breath and then squinted his eyes and looked up to the ever-darkening sky, as if searching for some technology god he could blame for his phone's shortcomings. All he ended up getting was snow in one of his nostrils.

He sighed and shoved his now-dead cell phone back in his pocket. He wondered if Leah had heard anything at all of what he'd said. He hoped so, because he was serious.

Earlier, before he'd joined Neil in the box truck, he'd told Leah that as soon as he knew where he was going, he'd tell her. And he would. He was ready. He'd come to the realization—not on his own, but with the help of friends (some living, some not) over the last couple of months—that it wasn't his job to protect her. At least not in the sense that he'd thought it was. Life was too short to shield yourself from those you loved, from those who made life worth living. Leah was a headstrong woman who could make her own decisions, take her own risks. It was not Lance's job, nor did he have the authority, to stop her.

Plus, he missed her desperately. And the feeling seemed to be reciprocated.

Despite a not-quite-dispelled feeling of uneasiness—because no matter what, Lance knew he was not done fighting the evil lurking in the shadows—he was excited to know that he wouldn't have to continue on alone forever.

There was her.

There was him.

And soon they would be them.

With a fresh burst of feel-good adrenaline, Lance pushed ahead through the snow. After what felt like an hour but was likely only twenty minutes, the sky was nearly black and another inch of snow had fallen—maybe more—and Lance's mood began to falter again. How far away was the town still? And could he make it there in the pitch black of the early night? Worse, if he were to freeze to death on the side of this road—or even in the middle of it—how long would it be before somebody found him?

And how would Leah ever know?

It was this last thought alone that propelled him faster. He tucked his head down against the wind and willed his legs to work harder. He wasn't in as good of shape as when he'd been a high school basketball star, but he still had some stamina to give.

This would not be the end. He knew that, deep down, even if the evidence seemed to suggest the contrary.

Ahead, fifty yards, maybe a bit more, the road curved to the right, disappearing around an outcropping of trees. With his head down the way it was, Lance hadn't noticed that the woods had been encroaching in, closer and closer to the road. Beyond the trees that filled out the curve in the road, there was the faint glow of yellow light.

Lance Brody, like a moth to a flame, nearly sprinted all the way to it. He rounded the bend in the road and stopped in his tracks, sneakers skidding in the snow.

He stared ahead, breathing hard, white plumes puffing from his mouth with each breath and vanishing into the night.

He'd found a motel.

[2]

IT WAS FULL DARK WHEN LANCE ROUNDED THE CORNER and found the motel. A black and starless sky above and the dull white of the snow-covered ground below.

The motel itself, a long single-story strip of building that resembled a discarded cigarette carton, ran parallel to the road, set back far enough to allow for a small parking lot that was just big enough for guests to nose their vehicles up to the front of their rooms—If there'd been any guests, that was. The parking lot was empty, a river of undisturbed snow that glowed almost yellow under the dim lights of the motel's overhang that ran along its front, giving *potential* guests protection from the elements as they ushered their bags to and from their vehicles. There were six rooms in total. Six closed doors. Six dark windows. At the far end of the building, beneath a tall utility pole with a makeshift spotlight shining down—this had been the light Lance had seen from the opposite side of the bend—was another room with an all-glass door and a bigger window than the rest. Behind this door and window, there was light. Warm and pleasant. In the window, a red neon sign read: OFFICE. A

Coke machine hummed just outside the office door, in between it and the first of the rooms for rent.

Lance stood in the middle of the road and took this all in, letting his eyes slide over the building from a distance as the snow continued to fall. A weathered marquee sign sat unevenly on the outskirts of the lot, just inside the cone of light cast by the spotlight. Plain black letters spelled: VACANCY.

Lance wondered when the last time somebody had needed to add the word NO to the sign had been. He took another look at the building, then up and down the forgotten road he was standing on, and assumed it had been a very, very long time.

Despite the glow of the lights, the sudden beacon presented to him on his unknown path, Lance's eyes kept searching the darkness that stretched in both directions on either side of him. He looked up and beyond the motel's roof, barely able to make out the tops of the trees, their branches swaying in the wind that still gusted and rushed at him.

There was a feeling of isolation that seemed all at once unnerving. But there was something else in the air, too. Something heavier. Something more akin to ... *desperation.*

It seemed to reach out from the row of darkened rooms and try to grab him, pull him in with an icy grip.

But maybe that was just the wind.

Maybe it wasn't.

Lance took a step closer to the motel, and when he felt the tingle at the base of his skull, the slight buzz that crept up his neck, he knew with great clarity that he'd been mistaken. It was not the town he was supposed to reach this evening. It was this place.

This motel.

The cold had chilled him to his bones, and the snow was only getting deeper. Without even the slightest concern as to why he was needed here, Lance Brody walked toward the motel's office. He could start to figure out the rest once he was warm again. He would pay large amounts of money for some coffee right now.

His sneakers shuffled through the snow as he crossed the last few feet of road, and then he stepped into the motel's parking lot and—

He woke up lying on his side with half his face buried in the snow. He sat up, gasping and spitting snow, brushing it from his face and neck and hair. His ears were ringing, almost painfully, as if they'd just popped after a huge elevation change, and his heart was thumping in his chest as if he'd had not just one cup of coffee but several pots. The motel was before him, blurred and swaying left and right, almost as if it were spinning. The individual lights recessed in the overhang heliographed and twinkled like stars.

A rush of nausea overcame him, and Lance closed his eyes tight and swallowed down sour bile rising in the back of this throat. He tried to calm himself, taking deep breaths of cold air and holding it in his lungs for a five count before exhaling and repeating.

Focus, Lance. Focus.

He focused on the clean air, the coldness of the snow beneath him, the sound of his own heart beating in his chest. He continued with his deep breathing and slowly the ringing in his ears subsided, the nausea passed. Finally, he opened his eyes and saw the motel had stopped moving and come back into focus.

The Coke machine still hummed, and all the windows except for the office were still dark.

Lance stood, slowly, and adjusted his backpack on his shoulders. Brushed the snow off the rest of him and then looked down at the half-assed snow-angel he'd managed to make when he'd collapsed.

What happened?

Standing in the parking lot, he turned and looked behind him, back to the road. He saw his own footprints in the snow, barely filled in at all, leading right to the place where he'd collapsed.

I wasn't out long, he thought. *Not if I can still see the prints so clearly.*

To further validate this thought, in a matter of seconds, he watched as the footprints began to vanish before his eyes, the heavily falling snow doing its best to erase all memory of Lance's travel.

He tried to think, tried to replay the last few moments in his memory and make sense of it. But there was nothing. One moment he'd started walking toward the motel's office, and the next he was on the ground.

A normal person—one without Lance's gifts and abilities—would probably become concerned about their own health, worry and fret about what sort of medical ailment they were suffering that would cause such a sudden collapse. But Lance did not ponder his heart or his brain or anything else, because he'd experienced these certain types of physical anomalies before in his lifetime—reactions to the Universe and spirit world sending him signals, issuing warnings.

The buzzing at the base of his skull was the most basic example of this.

But what had just happened ... it was different.

Powerful.

Lance had no idea what it meant, what he'd just been offered. But, as he looked down at the snow and watched as his footprints completely disappeared, he would be willing to bet his collapse had occurred at the exact moment he'd stepped off the road and touched the motel's parking lot.

Part of him wanted to walk back, cross the parking lot's

threshold and step back onto the road. But another part of him was not ready for another blast of whatever had just knocked him down for the count. And another part—a smaller part that was lurking deeper down, hiding behind the rest—was afraid to try for another reason.

What if he wasn't allowed to leave? What if something stopped him?

High on a dose of curiosity and fascination, while trying to ignore the bite of fear that accompanied it, Lance Brody turned and walked across the parking lot toward the office.

The marquee promised there was a vacancy, after all.

[3]

By the time he reached the door to the motel's office, Lance felt mostly normal again. The effects of his temporary blackout had faded away and he was able to suppress the coldness in the air from taking a front seat in his consciousness—not the cold from the snow and wind, mind you, but the coldness that seemed to radiate from the motel itself, the feeling that there was something here that needed him ... or wanted him. There was a difference, though both could be dangerous.

He stepped up onto the concrete walkway that ran along the front of the motel's rooms and stamped some of the snow from his shoes. Underneath the overhang, the snow was not as deep yet, but the wind was doing its best to blow the stuff in to remedy the situation, even things out. Lance passed the humming Coke machine and stood in front of the office door, taking a quick second to peer in through the glass.

For a moment, he flashed back to his first day in Westhaven, the day after his mother had died. It felt like a long time ago now. A very long time. That had been the first day of the rest of his life. An overused phrase, but accurate. The beginning of his journey that had no defined ending or purpose—none that he was aware of, that is. He'd walked along the sidewalks and roads of Westhaven that first day and had found himself in a very similar situation to this: finding a small motel, feeling its pull, walking into the office with no sense of expectation.

And he'd found Leah.

It was one of the worst days of his life, but also one of the best.

He'd lost so much, but he'd found something amazing.

How he *missed* her.

Lance shook the snow from his hoodie, pushed open the door, and walked inside the motel's office, ready to see what he'd find this time.

An old-fashioned bell hung above the office door and gave off a startling jingle when Lance pushed through it. Already on edge after the parking lot incident, Lance jumped at the noise and felt his heart slide up into his throat. In his anxiousness, he stepped directly over the floor mat just inside the threshold and his wet sneaker slid on the linoleum, causing him to do a bit of a half-split before he managed to reach out and grab the door and stop himself from getting a pulled groin. He righted himself, stood up fully, adjusted his backpack, and looked around to apologize to whoever might have witnessed his clumsiness.

But there was nobody there to see.

An L-shaped counter took up the entire left side of the room, with a ledger book, a banker's lamp, a small bell, and stacks of assorted pamphlets and papers organized neatly across it. A bowl of peppermint candies was half-empty—the only thing that looked *alive* on the counter aside from the glowing bulb in the small lamp. On the wall behind the counter were a framed business license, and a large calendar—a Norman Rock-well-esque painting of a family sitting down to what looked like Thanksgiving dinner above the November days and weeks. Somebody had been using a red marker to X off each day that had passed. To the right of the calendar was a wooden pegboard with six brass hooks in need of a good polishing. Keys hung from each hook, attached to large plastic key chains labeled with faded black numbers. Numbers one through six. A key for each room. All keys were accounted for. Past the pegboard, there was a closed door leading to a back room with the word PRIVATE painted in black.

On the back wall was an open door leading into a dark hole in which Lance could just make out the silhouette of a toilet and sink, and along the right, opposite the counter, were a water-cooler, the jug atop also half-full, just like the bowl of candies, and a row of metal folding chairs that could have been brand-new or a hundred years old—the same ambiguous kind you find at every church potluck or grade-school assembly in rural America. The wood paneling on the walls and the peeling linoleum flooring told the story of how long it'd been since the place had been remodeled.

But it was not an altogether unpleasant space. It smelled clean, if not without a hint of mildew, and the baseboard heating hummed and choked along well enough to keep it warm.

Compared to walking along for miles in the whipping snow and freezing cold, the motel's office might have been paradise.

"Is it you?"

A woman's voice, soft and full of wonder.

"Is it *really* you?"

Lance spun back toward the counter and saw that the PRIVATE door was cracked open, enough for half a face to stare back at him from behind it. As soon as he turned, the door opened fully and quickly, and a small older woman walked out and greeted him.

"Hello there, and welcome. Can I help you?"

She was short and thin, with long gray hair that hung down to the middle of her back. She wore faded blue jeans and a heavy sweater and snow boots that clopped loudly on the floor as she made her way to the counter. Up close, her face showed her age more so than the rest of her, for while she moved quickly on her feet, her skin was wrinkled and liver-spotted. Her eyes were squinting against the light of the banker's lamp, and the red from the neon OFFICE sign in the window illuminated her right side, giving her an almost two-faced glow. She smiled at him, a small grin that Lance thought was meant to be friendly, but seemed a bit disappointed, as well.

"Hi," Lance said, smiling back. "What is it you asked me?"

"Can I help you?"

Lance shook his head. "No, before that. I thought I heard you ask something else. Just before you came out from the door."

The woman smiled a bigger grin, raised her eyebrows and shrugged her shoulders. "I don't think so. Must have been the ghosts."

Lance's face fell, and the woman noticed, immediately backpedaling with her words. "Goodness, I'm only fooling. Forgive me. Just a joke. Wouldn't be very good for business if I went around telling customers we had ghosts around here, now would it? Trust me. Been there, done that."

Lance said nothing. A strong gust of wind slammed into the motel, rattling the window. Lance and the woman both turned and looked out the glass as snow danced through the air.

"Let me try again," the woman started. "My name is Meriam. Welcome to my motel. Would you like a room for the night, or are you here to sell something?" She eyed him up and down, then added, "I'm guessing a room, right? You don't seem quite the traveling salesman type, and if you were, you'd be bad at your job, because any half-witted fool can look at this place and know I ain't the kind to be spending money on things we don't need."

Lance's brain worked to try and figure out what was happening. He had clearly heard the woman speak before she'd come out from the door. *Is it really you?* she'd asked. But now she was obviously trying to ignore the question and push on to change the subject.

Or maybe it was the ghosts, Lance thought. But that didn't feel right. Not this time.

Maybe she's just old and senile.

Okay, now that's just rude, he scolded himself. *Mom would be very disappointed.*

The memory of his mother took him away for a second, his mind floating back to his hometown. When he snapped out of it, Meriam was waiting patiently, but Lance could see something else in her eyes. Something akin to suspicion ... or maybe it was plain curiosity.

"A room, please," Lance said. "I was trying to make it to town but got caught in the snow."

"Seemed to come out of nowhere, didn't it?" Meriam said, flipping open the ledger book and writing the day's date on the next blank line. "Wasn't even in the forecast. But since when do those weather fools ever get it right?"

Lance said nothing.

"Name?" Meriam asked.

"Lance Brody."

In very careful and deliberate penmanship, she wrote his name next to the date in the ledger book and then looked it over, as if checking for typos. "Rate's thirty-five a night," she said, looking up. "You got cash?"

Lance nodded. "Yes, ma'am."

"Okay. I prefer that, so I don't have to pay the flippin' fees for the charge cards. Every dollar counts these days, don't you know? And everybody wants to try and take it from you."

Lance nodded again, pulling the cash from his pocket and laying two twenties on the counter. Meriam scooped them up and stuffed them in the pocket of her own pants—which Lance thought odd but was too confused to worry much about—and didn't offer him any change. Then she turned and reached up to the pegboard and grabbed key number one from its hook. "Room one okay? It's right next door."

And while Lance's eyes had watched her reach for the key, it was then that he'd noticed something else about the pegboard that he'd not seen from farther away when he'd first entered the office. All the keys were identical, as were all the hooks, but at the far-right end, on the very last hook, the key to room six stood out. The printed black 6 on the plastic key chain was much darker and more legible than the rest of the numbers on the other keys. Lance could maybe have assumed the key chain had been replaced more recently than the others, but the tangle of cobwebs that were just visible in the dim light cast across the wall, visible only on key number six, looping and twisting around it and its key chain and hook, told a different story.

Given the location of the motel and the quality of the accommodations, Lance would wager that none of the rooms here got much traffic, but it was obvious that room six had not been used for a very long time.

"Actually," Lance said, just as Meriam was sliding the key to room one across the counter to him, "would it be possible to have room six? I like being on the end."

Meriam stopped moving and looked up to him, her eyes meeting his and staying there, imploring him for something more. She looked … hopeful?

Her eyes narrowed and she cocked her head slowly to the side, her long gray hair splaying out in a fan. "Who are you?"

Lance had no idea what was happening, which was not exactly out of the ordinary. But one thing he tried not to allow himself to do was to speak without knowing what he was saying, or who he was saying it to.

"You know, I get that a lot," he said. "I must look like a movie star or a famous athlete or something like that." He offered a small chuckle and then shrugged. "But I'm just Lance. Sorry."

Whatever place the woman's mind had gone to, she reeled herself back quickly, just as she'd done earlier. "Room six is not available, I'm afraid."

And that was all.

Lance smiled and took the key to room one from the counter. "No worries. This'll be fine, I'm sure. Thank you very much."

"If you need anything," Meriam said, just as Lance's hand had found the door to head back outside, "just dial zero on the phone. It'll ring me up here."

Lance nodded and said another thank-you and then pulled open the door and stepped back into the snow.

What I really need is some answers.

[4]

Stepping back outside was a bit like getting hit by a bus. As soon as Lance's sneakers touched the ground and the office door closed behind him, a steamroller of a gust of wind rushed at him like a defensive tackle and hit him full force, nearly knocking him off his feet. Lance grunted, slipped slightly in the snow, and then turned and shuffled the short way down the sidewalk to the door to room one.

But not before glancing over his shoulder and seeing Meriam still behind the counter, watching him as he went.

Even through the snow that peppered Lance's vision, even though the panes of glass, even at such a distance, the look she was giving him was unmistakable. She'd worked to hide it while he'd been directly in front of her, covering it with different, less apparent emotions. But now, Lance thought he recognized the look on Meriam's face for what it truly was.

The look of somebody who'd just seen a ghost.

Lance fumbled with the key chain, which nearly snatched from his hand by the wind, and finally slid the brass key into its home. There was a satisfying click of the tumblers in the lock and Lance turned the knob and pushed the door open, thinking about what Meriam had said to him earlier—*Must have been the ghosts.*

Not the best thought for a normal person to have as they entered a dark motel room off a stretch of desolate road. But for Lance, it was more of an irritant. Because if there were ghosts at the motel, he wished they'd go ahead and show themselves so he could get started with whatever it was he was meant to do here.

Lance figured there was more going on in Meriam's head than she wanted to admit to him, and rightfully so, Lance being a complete stranger and all. But her words—the words Lance knew he had heard her ask before she'd slipped out from the door behind the counter—were what made him most curious.

Is it really you?

It was as if she'd been waiting for somebody. Waiting for him?

But why the quick change, the sudden dismissiveness?

Lance sighed. Closed the motel room's door, shutting out the wind and the cold, and felt along the wall for a light switch.

He found one, switched it on.

Nothing happened.

He flipped it up and down a few times and then gave up, sighing even heavier. For the room to be as pitch black as it was, there must be curtains drawn shut across the window, he reasoned, so he took a careful step sideways and reached out with his hand and felt the rough, almost sticky fabric of drapes that were likely older than he was. He gripped a handful of the stuff and tried to push it away from him along its track, but it didn't budge. It needed to slide in the opposite direction.

Lance took a step forward, meaning to follow the curtain fabric until he found the other end, and his knee connected with something low and hard. A table, presumably, connected with what must have been a chair, causing a clattering of wood as the things wobbled back into place. Lance, rubbing his knee with one hand, swung his backpack off his shoulder and set it gently where he thought the tabletop should be. Then he unzipped a small front pouch and felt around inside until he found the tiny flashlight. He pulled it out and clicked it on.

There was a dead woman hanging from a bedsheet at the back of the room.

Lance jumped, surprise rocking him back, his left arm and shoulder getting tangled in the drapes. He fought to get it free, and when he did, he shined the flashlight directly on the body. The woman's face was puffy and swollen, her skin purple, deep bruising along the bottom of her jawline and neck where the bedsheet wrapped tight and had dug in. She wore flannel pajamas, her bare feet sticking out, toes pointed down, swaying ever so gently, as if she'd only recently ended her life.

When her eyes shot open, Lance actually let out a small grunt.

Then she spoke, her voice raspy and low, but clear all the same, as if she were whispering directly into Lance's ear.

"*He'll be waiting,*" she said.

And then the lights turned on and she was gone.

Must have been the ghosts.

Meriam's words echoed in Lance's head as he stood by the small wooden table by the window and looked across the motel room to where the woman had been.

No, he thought, *she'd only been joking. A nervous cover-up because she didn't want to admit to me that she'd really said something else.*

It was simply a gut feeling he had. A feeling he could trust. There *were* ghosts at the motel—at least one, that was—but Meriam had not seen them. Lance had picked up no trace of any sort of vibe coming off the woman, no sensation that she possessed any type of gifts other than hospitality management, and that was generous, if he was being honest.

But still ... there'd been *something* in her eyes. That much he couldn't deny.

And now the dead woman in his room.

Lance was beginning to think that his default state of mind was permanently set to confused.

His stomach growled. He'd not eaten since the fast-food drive-thru Neil had stopped at for lunch several hours ago. Lance unzipped a side pouch of his backpack and pulled out a pack of peanut butter crackers. Opened them, popped the first cracker into his mouth whole, and then surveyed the room.

Small wooden table with a chair on either side (painful to bump your knee on). Two full-size beds with forest-green comforters and chipped wooden headboards, nightstand in between them with two reading lamps and a beige plastic telephone. A long dresser opposite the beds with a big boxy television set centered on it. Framed photographs on the walls showing scenes of mountains and forests and rivers, probably local.

Everything was old and worn, but it looked clean enough—even the brown carpet didn't have too many stains—and Lance would even go so far as to call it cozy. You know, if you could overlook the occasional dead person.

Lance tossed another cracker into his mouth and walked past the front of the beds toward the rear of the room, where he'd seen her. There was a wide alcove cut out from the main living space that held a long vanity with two sinks and a mirror. It was darkened, and Lance reached just inside and found a light switch on the wall by a door that led to the toilet and shower. A row of fluorescents sputtered to life above him. He looked up and saw the decorative wooden latticework that protruded from the ceiling, helping to separate the two spaces. It was through this that the woman had tied her sheet. It was right here, right where Lance was standing, that she had decided to die.

But for now, all looked normal.

Lance reached up with a long arm and touched the wood where the sheet had been tied, disturbed dust floating down into his eyes. He waited a beat, but the dust was all he was going to get. No visions, no feelings, just wood and dust and the dead woman's words lingering in his head.

After a quick peek into the little room with the shower and toilet, Lance left the fluorescents burning and made his way back to the table. He sat in one of the wooden chairs and quickly took care of the rest of his crackers, washing them down with a bottle of water. Considering the storm and his current location, he was very glad he'd stocked up on a few supplies at the little roadside store when he'd met Neil. He'd bought the supplies right before Leah had called him.

Remembering the phone call, Lance pulled his phone from his pocket and then his charger from his backpack. He found an outlet on the wall behind the table and plugged it in, hoping the old wiring was sound. He still felt responsible for one motel burning down. He didn't want to add another to the list.

After a few minutes, the little screen on the front of the phone lit up and Lance quickly snatched it from the table and flipped it open. Scrolled to Leah's contact and called her. But when he pressed the phone to his ear, nothing happened.

Silence.

Not even any tone or beep or recording letting him know his call could not be completed.

He pulled the phone away from his head and looked at the reception bars, and of course, there were none. Not even the little mocking one.

Frustrated, he tossed the phone onto the table harder than he'd meant to, and the battery popped off the back. He took a deep breath and tried to calm himself before reassembling his flip phone. He was letting his emotions get the best of him too frequently these days. He couldn't go and break his only lifeline to the outside world. His only connection to Leah and Marcus Johnston and...

They were all. The only people left who he was close to. He knew his mother would always be with him—the memory of her and her wisdom and guidance. But in terms of human beings who were alive that he could reach out and touch and feel and smell and speak to and laugh with and share an experience with ... he did not like being so alone.

One step at a time, Lance.

His mother was the most patient person he'd ever known. He would do his best to be more like her now.

With nowhere to go and nobody to talk to and no idea what to do, Lance found the brick-sized remote to the television and turned it on. Found a syndicated episode of *Full House* and started to watch, his eyes occasionally glancing over toward the alcove, waiting to see if the dead woman would come back.

He fell asleep thinking about what it must be like to live in a house full of so many people to care about you.

[5]

A THUNDEROUS POUNDING ON THE MOTEL ROOM DOOR woke him.

Three powerful knocks that shook the door on its hinges and rattled the windows struck home directly in Lance's skull.

His eyes shot open and he jumped up. Ready to spring into action and...

And what?

He didn't know. But what he did know was that nobody knocks that hard unless there's trouble. Unless something bad is about to happen or about to be said.

Three more knocks. This time loud enough to make him reach up and cover his ears. Forceful enough that he nearly fell backward, back onto the bed.

Wait, he thought. *Impossible that somebody knocking could...*

But he stopped himself. Lance knew better than to use the word impossible. It shouldn't exist in his vocabulary.

He lowered his hands from his ears and stood still, the room all at once silent. Slowly, he stepped forward and found the edge of the curtain and eased it back just enough to look out the—

There was no window behind the drapes. Only a solid wall of the same wood paneling as the rest of the room. Lance ripped the curtain all the way aside and stood back, staring at the wall. His mind working to make sense of it.

Then another knock sent his heart into overdrive and jump-started his body. He walked to the door and looked through the peephole. Saw only blackness.

Somebody's covering it.

Not good.

Lance glanced to the phone on the nightstand. Meriam had told him to dial zero if he needed anything. He wondered how much time he had. How long would it be before the person (or thing?) outside the door grew impatient and simply entered of their own accord. Did he have time to get to the phone and make the call? And if he did, what could Meriam really do? Call the police? They'd never make it in time.

So it was then that Lance Brody made the decision to do what he usually found himself doing: trusting the Universe, trusting himself, being brave, and facing the problem head-on.

Without warning, he gripped the doorknob, turned it, and flung the door open. Jumped back, ready for ... well, anything.

He froze.

His gaze fixed out the opened door on what lay beyond.

He squinted, then closed his eyes fully. Counted to five and opened them again.

Eased himself closer to the door, cautiously, still expecting an assault of some sort.

Nothing happened. Nothing attacked, except the scene before him attacking all his rationality and understanding.

Lance was looking at the very same motel he was currently standing inside.

It was a view he was familiar with, because what could only have been a couple hours ago, he'd been standing in the middle of the road and getting his first glimpse of the motel from the exact same vantage point he was seeing from through his room's door.

Impossible.

There was that word again. The one he shouldn't use, creeping its way into his thoughts.

He tampered down the ridicule and forced himself to think, to analyze what he was seeing as somebody with his abilities, his understanding (or lack thereof) of the Universe and its rules.

Quickly, the scene before him became clearer.

It was a message. A clue. Possibly a warning.

Lance reached a hand outside his door, letting it cross the threshold to see what would happen. The cold air bit and the wind gusted, but his hand remained attached to his body, so he considered that a good sign.

He took a breath and stepped outside.

An ear-popping *whoosh* sucked the air from behind him, and when Lance spun back around, his motel room was gone. There was just the darkness of the field and trees on the opposite side of the road, all smeared by the white flurries of snow.

Lance shivered at the sudden exposure to the cold and the wind. He turned around, finding himself standing exactly in the same spot he'd been earlier when he'd arrived from his long walk along the road.

The lights were still burning in the office window. The spotlight still shone down and tried to illuminate the parking lot. All the rooms remained darkened. Closed off and ominous.

But Lance was not paying attention to any of this.

There were people standing in front of some of the motel's rooms.

Well, that wasn't exactly true. There were the silhouettes of people in front of every room, semi-amorphous figures that were filled with what looked like fuzzy television static, blanking out any distinct features other than human shapes.

And beside each figure or group of figures in front of each motel room door was a boy.

More a young man, really, this boy. Lance squinted against the snow and used one hand to shield his eyes from some of the spotlight's glare. The carbon copy of the boy stood by each door with the corresponding fuzzy-television people, like somebody had performed a computer copy-and-paste. He was fairly tall and lean, wearing baggy blue jeans and an oversized knit sweater. He had stocking cap pulled down low over his ears and—

He looks like me, Lance realized.

Not identical. Not by a long shot. Especially when the boy turned and Lance could make out the cleft chin and the flat cheekbones and the pointed nose. But in terms of physical stature and build ... the replicated boy standing by the motel rooms' doors could have very easily been mistaken for Lance from a distance, and especially from behind.

The copy of the boy that was standing with a solo figure in front of door one reached out and embraced the static image of a human in a hug. At the boy's touch, the silhouette quickly faded into color, its features emerging like a butterfly from a cocoon.

It was the woman Lance had seen hanging from the bedsheet. The one who'd spoken her mysterious message and then vanished.

Here and now, wherever and whenever here and now was, she looked much more alive. Cheeks rosy from the cold and plumes of breath billowing from her mouth as she spoke into the frosted air. After her embrace with the boy, she turned and entered room one.

Lance watched as the boy in front of the other rooms' doors

likewise embraced the people he was with and allowed their bodies to take full form. There was a middle-aged couple at room two, and a child—a girl, no more than eleven or twelve—at room five.

And then Lance's heart went cold and the lights seemed to darken and in a flash of something that wasn't actually something at all, there was suddenly only one person left in front of the motel. In front of room six.

Lance Brody stood in the middle of the road that should have been the walkway outside his motel room and stared back at himself.

This time, he was sure of it. This lone figure who remained while all the fuzzy-television people and copies of the boy had vanished was him. It was wearing the same outfit as Lance was now, cargo shorts and his favorite hoodie.

But Lance was here. He reached down and patted his chest and legs and felt his head, just to make sure.

And if he was here, he could not be there, right?

Lance on the road stood completely still, not even breathing as he watched Lance by the motel room.

The other Lance was also standing still, staring straight ahead, looking out across the parking lot directly in front of room six. The two Lances stood that way for a moment, and then the Lance in front of the motel room suddenly shifted his eyes upward, out toward the road. Fixed them directly on the spot where Lance was standing.

And then he waved.

And for some reason, Lance felt very much like it was the wave of somebody saying goodbye.

The Lance by the motel room turned around and reached out for the handle to room six, and just as the Lance on the road opened his mouth to call and out and tell this other Lance to wait, there was another *whoosh*, this time all around him and—

Lance sat up, his heart pounding and ears ringing, and called out, "Wait!"

But he was back in his motel room. Safely atop the bed with the television still playing and the heat still humming from the baseboards and the lights still on.

Still alone.

[6]

ON THE SMALL TELEVISION SCREEN, *FULL HOUSE*
continued on with Uncle Joey saying something that Lance
didn't hear, which caused Uncle Jesse to give an eye roll, which
caused the laugh track to roar, which caused Lance to get up
from the bed and cross the room and switch the television off.
He'd enjoyed the white noise of the show earlier, but now, with
his mind racing and his heart still coming down off its high, he
wanted to eliminate distractions. He wanted quiet. Needed it.
Because confusion was grabbing him by the wrists and ankles
and trying to drag him away, pull him down into a stupor of
disbelief.

And not because of the fuzzy-television people, and not
even because of the copy-and-paste boy—the boy who might
have been him at a quick glance from behind—but because of
the last thing he'd seen.

Himself.

Lance replayed that last bit of the scene over and over in his
head, watched as the other version of himself had stared, seemingly perplexed, at something the current version of himself had
not been able to see, right before something like recognition had

flickered across the other version of Lance's face, and he'd shifted his head and raised his eyes and stared.

Stared directly at Lance and then waved.

It was that last bit that bothered Lance. The way that the Dream-Lance—and at this point, Lance was calling the entire episode a dream, for lack of a more accurate word—had seemed to know that the real Lance was there and had essentially said goodbye before he'd turned to enter room six.

Goodbye was a word that carried many different weights. It could be casual and light as a feather, such as saying goodbye to a coworker before you left work for the day, or at the end of a phone call with a friend. But it could also be burdensome, a two-ton boulder that crushed lives and destroyed families.

Lance thought about the dead woman he'd seen hanging from the bedsheet, and the alive version of her from his dream.

She'd said the ultimate goodbye, in the worst possible way.

Which sort of goodbye had the Dream-Lance used? What was going to happen inside room six once he stepped inside?

And to Lance, the most important and troubling question of all was this: was the dream nothing more than a message from the Universe to be interpreted, a clue to be used in a greater mystery, or was it more? Glimpses of what had already been, and also what might be? A hint at things to come coupled with flashes of the past, all meshed together in some sort of hybrid vision?

Lance shook his head and shifted his thoughts. Changed course and sailed his mind away from the image of Dream-Lance and headed toward another point of curiosity. The copy-and-paste boy.

Lance looked at the beige plastic phone on the nightstand. Remembered Meriam's words. *Is it really you?*

Lance sat on the bed and picked up the phone and pressed zero. It rang once before she answered.

"Yes?"

"Hello, ma'am. I'm sorry if I woke you," Lance said, though judging by how quickly Meriam had answered the phone, he knew he hadn't. It was almost as if she'd been waiting for his call. "And I know this might sound strange, but I ... well, I have some questions."

There was a pause. Short, but long enough for Lance to know she was thinking about what the best course of action was. Then she said, "Do you like coffee?"

The walk from room one to the motel's office was just as short as it'd been earlier but seemingly twice as cold. The snow had blown up onto the walkway beneath the overhang, and there was at least an inch of accumulation there. Lance left footprints large enough to entice big game hunters, or maybe Bigfoot enthusiasts, as he crossed the short distance with his hood pulled tight around his face and his hand tucked into the front pouch of his sweatshirt.

The wind howled, and the cold scratched at his skin.

He'd felt the cold during his dream, certain it had been the real thing, but now he was quickly reminded of just how vicious the weather had gotten. The dream had been a good imitation, but nothing compared to the real deal.

Wasn't even in the forecast.

Lance Brody did not get cold, not in the sense that most people did. He had no problems wearing shorts year-round, and he found it much more uncomfortable to be overly warm than overly cool. This had been an issue in his and his mother's home during the winter months. They were constantly playing an unofficial game of dueling thermostat settings.

So the fact that Lance found himself growing so cold now,

after such a few short steps from his room to the door to the motel's office, sparked a small debate in his mind.

Am I just unaccustomed to weather this far north? Which wasn't completely out of the question, considering he'd spent nearly his entire life living in Virginia before being forced to move on a few short months ago. Or...

Or is this something else, this cold? Is this something more than you'd find on The Weather Channel?

Lance risked a glance up into the wind, toward the road.

There'd been the blackout, him sitting up in the snowy parking lot with no memory of ever going down. There'd been Meriam's odd behavior. There'd been the dead woman in his room. There'd been the dream.

Wasn't even in the forecast.

Lance freed a hand from his hoodie and pushed open the office door.

Meriam was waiting for him, standing behind the counter and urging to him to shut the door before he let the heat out. Lance caught the door as it began to swing closed behind him and helped it along, pushing it shut against the wind. Then he turned and basked in the glory that was the warmth of the office, feeling himself instantly begin to thaw out, the snow on his sneakers quickly melting to small puddles on the floor.

He wiped his feet on the doormat and Meriam said, "Come on around the counter here." She pointed to the far end, where the counter opened along the wall. "Coffee's in the back."

Right then and there, Lance would have agreed to accompany Frodo to Mordor to destroy the ring if it meant a big hot cup of coffee in return. He walked across the office and joined Meriam behind the counter, where she gave him one final appraising glance up and down before pushing through the door she'd come through earlier when Lance had checked in. She motioned for him to follow.

At first sight, it reminded Lance of a room in a retirement home or assisted living facility. One large rectangular space segmented into all the comforts of home. He was standing in a carpeted living space with a faded blue love seat and recliner positioned in front of an old boxy television set with a modern cable box atop it. There was a coffee table with books stacked neatly, and a small bookshelf tucked away in the corner with framed photographs on the shelves. To his right, the direction where Meriam had gone, was a kitchen with a two-top table against the wall and a long counter with a sink, microwave, oven, and, most importantly, coffeemaker.

There was another door beside the kitchen that must have led to a bedroom and bath.

She lives here, Lance thought.

And then he thought of Leah. How she'd had her own bedroom in the back of her and her dad's motel that she'd managed.

Before it'd burned down.

The coffeemaker, a small black plastic thing that was so simple it only needed a single on/off switch, sputtered and gurgled and then sighed, and Meriam pulled two mugs down from a cabinet and poured.

"Cream or sugar?" she asked over her shoulder.

"No, thank you. Black is fine, ma'am."

She made a sound that might have been a suppressed scoff. Shook her head as she spooned helpings of sugar from a small glass jar into her own mug. "My husband drank it black. Sometimes I wonder if men have any taste buds at all."

Lance didn't know what to say to that.

Meriam turned and set both mugs down on the kitchen table. Sat in the chair facing the living room and waved for Lance to join her. Lance pushed the sleeves of his sweatshirt up around his elbows, surprised at how quickly he'd gone from freezing to overly warm, and pulled the other chair from the table and sat. The baseboard heating hummed at his feet.

"I appreciate the coffee, ma'am," he said, taking a sip that turned into a gulp, that turned into him downing half the mug before he came up for air. It was too hot, burning his throat, but it was good all the same. Sometimes simple is all you need.

After he'd set the mug back down, Meriam stared at him as if she'd just witnessed a magic trick she was trying to figure out in her head, blinked a few times, then jerked her head back toward the counter and the coffeemaker. "You're welcome. Feel free to help yourself when you need more. I'm always brewin' it. I got insomnia, you see. Almost never sleep, so the coffee helps me keep on going. Nice to have some company for a change."

Lance nodded. "Thank you, ma'am."

"And stop with all the 'ma'am' talk. I appreciate that you're trying to be polite, but point taken. Speak freely, boy. This isn't a test."

Lance wondered about that. Because despite Meriam's feigned ignorance thus far, all signs were currently pointed to this little late-night coffee rendezvous being very much a test of who could get what information out of who first, and not just a friendly social visit between an insomnia-suffering lady and the young stranger who'd wandered on foot into her motel.

On the phone, Lance had said he had questions.

And Meriam had not even asked what they might be about. There'd been the pause, that moment where Lance figured she was contemplating just what she might be getting herself into, and then she'd invited him over.

She's just as curious as I am, Lance thought. *Just as curious about me as I am about this place.*

"Yes, ma'am," Lance said, then caught himself. "I mean ... yes. Okay. I'll try. But old habits die hard. My mother raised me right, you might say."

Meriam gave a small smile and nodded her head. "I think I do believe that. She certainly fed you right, tall as you are." She sipped her coffee. "Where is she these days? Back home, wherever that is?"

Lance felt that familiar twinge in his heart, let it hit and then waited for it to dissipate before he brought himself to answer. "She died. A few months ago."

He downed the rest of his coffee and stood to get more.

When he sat back down, Meriam said, "I'm very sorry about your mother. I would never have asked if I'd known."

Lance nodded a thank-you and sipped his fresh cup. Meriam sipped hers, and it was as if all of a sudden they both realized they could no longer hide the reason they'd come together. The small talk was quickly over, and now all it would take was one of them deciding to lead the charge.

It turned out to be Meriam.

She set her coffee mug on the table, folded her hands in her lap and looked Lance in the eye. "You want to know about the woman who died in your room, don't you?"

[7]

LANCE BRODY HAD SPENT HIS ENTIRE LIFE WITH THE ability to know things in ways that nobody would understand. Whether by premonition or by touch or by gut instinct or by the whispers of the dead who had not yet passed on, information that regular people would never ascertain without more direct methods flowed freely to Lance. It was one of his gifts. One of his burdens.

It was extremely useful, he had to admit. Even if sometimes he felt a flicker of guilt at invading somebody's private thoughts and memories.

So when Meriam asked her question—*You want to know about the woman who died in your room, don't you?*—Lance had a small moment of panic where he wondered if she was inside his head. If she, too, possessed some sort of extra sense that allowed her to see into his mind, read his thoughts.

It reminded him of the first day he'd seen the Reverend and the Surfer. The way the Reverend had let Lance pass by on the sidewalk and turn the corner before blasting his message into Lance's head, loud and as clear as if he'd been speaking directly into his ear. It had been jarring, frightening, sickening.

Lance considered this for a moment, adding up the suspicious looks Meriam had given him when he'd arrived, as if she knew secrets about him, and now this question that seemed very unlikely for her to have guessed.

Calm down, Lance. Slow it down and talk to her.

But, instead of denying it, or dancing around the subject, he decided to be direct. Honest.

"How did you know?" he asked, taking a casual sip of coffee.

Meriam gave him a look that Lance felt carried silent meaning, as if she knew they were both playing the game, but then her face shifted and she smiled and waved a dismissive hand in the air. "You're not the first who's come through here because of the rumors. But I must say, it's been a while. Several years, in fact. Longer, actually. It happened so long ago."

She eyed him again, another appraising up-and-down glance. "Before you were born, most likely."

"What happened?"

Meriam shot him a sly look. "You don't already know?"

Lance said nothing.

Meriam shrugged. "That poor woman ended her life." She shook her head. "So sad. Very, very sad. My husband was the one who found her. When she didn't check out that morning, he went to make sure everything was okay, and well ... it wasn't. It shook us both, badly."

"Did you know her?" Lance asked.

Meriam took a very small sip of coffee. "No. She'd only checked in two days before. Said she was visiting relatives in town. Had come up for a long weekend. Which sounded plausible, of course."

"Plausible? You mean, that's not why she was here?"

Meriam shook her head. "We found out later she had no family in the entire state. She was a single mother from North Carolina, and that's where all her relatives still were."

"So she drove several states away just to take her life? Why?"

Meriam was quiet for maybe a full minute before she answered. "According to the police, her three-year-old son had been missing for nearly a month. The search hadn't turned up anything—nothing she was satisfied with, anyway—and apparently she decided to take matters into her own hands."

"So she was looking for him here?"

Meriam shook her head. Shrugged again. "We never had any idea why she ended up here. Or why she picked our motel to kill herself."

She's lying, Lance thought. He didn't know how he knew, but something tugged at the back of his mind.

"Police never said anything else?"

"Why would they tell us? We weren't family. We were just a crime scene, essentially. We learned what everybody else learned, from the newspaper. We just wanted to move on. It killed business for nearly two months. Nobody would come near the place."

Lance processed this, then asked, "You mentioned rumors."

Meriam sat back in her chair, as if happy to move away from details of the suicide and discuss other things she felt more comfortable with. "Ah yes, the rumors. The very kind I'm sure that brought *you* here tonight. Because, let's face it"—she held out her hands and motioned to the space around her—"we aren't exactly the Hilton. What other reason would you have to be here?"

That's what I'm trying to figure out.

"Humor me," Lance said. "What are the rumors?"

In a very robotic voice, like somebody repeating something they've memorized and are forced to recite on a regular basis, Meriam said, "That the spirit of the woman who killed herself never checked out. That she haunts room one and chooses very inappropriate times to frighten my guests and make for great stories for ghost hunters and boggers to write about and make videos."

"Boggers?"

"Yes, those people who write articles on the Internet."

"I think it's *bloggers*, but I'm not exactly technically advanced. I still have a flip phone."

"Well, that makes two of us."

"Well," Lance said with a smile, "wouldn't being a niche tourist attraction actually *help* business?"

Meriam spoke sternly. "We are not a tourist attraction, we're a motel."

Lance said nothing.

Meriam shifted in her seat again and continued. "Anyway, one middle-aged door-to-door salesman started the rumor about six months after the initial accident, so roughly four months after things had started going back to normal. He sold encyclopedias, you see. Do you know what those are?"

Lance nodded.

"Well, he had his current inventory in his room. Said he didn't trust thieves not to break into his car to steal them." Meriam chuckled and rolled her eyes. "Like he was peddling record players or marijuana. Alas, he said he woke up in the middle of the night and all his books were floating around the room, spinning and spiraling, and then they all flew directly at him, like an attack. Said they busted up his face pretty well and good. And yeah, he had a black eye and busted lip and a bit of blood dried on his nostrils, but you know what else he had? You know what my husband found when he went in the room? An empty bottle of whiskey and only one dirty glass."

Lance nodded. "He got drunk and somehow hurt himself."

"Clearly. But apparently he was ignorant or prideful enough to fail to admit this and ended up making up a ghost story instead. When a few local folks over at the diner showed a bit of interest in his story over breakfast, he took it and ran with it. News spread fast. Like wildfire, as the saying goes." Meriam shrugged, as if Lance could work out the rest on his own. "And here we are."

Lance nodded again. "You and your husband have never seen anything to make you believe the room might actually be haunted?"

She gave him a stern look. "Goodness, you really are one of them, aren't you?"

Lance said nothing. Shrugged.

Meriam sighed. "No. We never did. My husband went to his grave still angry at that guy for starting such a bunch of baloney. After all we struggled with over the years, after all the... well, he never forgave the guy. This was all we had, you see? This motel, this was *ours*. It's what we worked and lived for. It was *everything* to us. And one down-on-his-luck fool tried to destroy it because he was a drunk and enjoyed the attention."

"I'm sorry," Lance said. "About your husband. And about all the rest."

Meriam was quiet for a bit and then nodded her thanks. She took a sip of coffee.

Lance's mind spun wildly, trying to figure out how to delicately shift the conversation, get more answers. Meriam liked to talk, despite her outward disposition.

His thoughts kept returning to the copy-and-paste boy. The one he'd seen hugging the woman who would eventually hang herself.

He asked, "Did she have any visitors?"

Meriam's eyes narrowed. "Who?"

"The lady who hanged herself in room one."

"I never told you how she ended her life."

Ah, so we are still playing the game. Good to know. Lance shrugged, "Rumors and boggers, remember?"

"Did you have somebody in mind? Someone you think might have visited a complete stranger from four states away, with no family or known friends in the area, at a rural mom-and-pop motel?"

Now Lance sat back in his chair, crossed his arms. He wasn't sure if in Meriam's curiosity about him, she was leaning toward him being friend or foe, but he guessed their conversation was reaching its end, and there was no sense in being indirect.

"A man, perhaps? You and your husband never saw *anyone* stop by the room while she was here? Not even a pizza delivery guy?"

The look Meriam gave Lance was so cold he had to pull down the sleeves of his hoodie.

"No," she said. "She was always alone. She died alone. God rest her soul."

"Did you figure out who it was you thought I looked like?"

"I'm sorry?"

Lance's last words came out with a bit more emphasis than he had intended, but he was becoming slowly frustrated with Meriam's withholding of information. Which he could not exactly prove, of course, but Lance had grown to trust his gut feelings pretty well. And in his experience, people who withheld information—*lied*, to put a finer point on it—usually were guilty of something. Didn't always mean it was something big, but something, all the same.

"When I checked in," Lance said. "You seemed like you confused me with somebody else, maybe? Did you ever figure out who it was?"

This was a test in its own right, from Lance's perspective. When he'd first entered the motel's office, he'd heard Meriam

56

ask, almost to herself, *Is it really you?* As if she thought Lance might be somebody she knew. She'd quickly denied it when he'd questioned her, but later, after Lance had asked for room six, she'd given him one of those appraising looks and asked, *Who are you?* A question that didn't imply she recognized him but that she was suddenly very aware that there was a lot more to him than what was on the surface. His inquiry about room six had triggered it, but why?

So, Lance wanted to see which one of those two questions she'd answer. Would she still deny the first completely, or would she slip up and give him something?

But all she said was, "No."

And that was that.

And then, "But I will ask again," she started, "who are you?"

Lance picked up his mug and drank the rest of his coffee and smiled. "I'm just a guy who needed a room to get out of the storm, and who very much appreciates your coffee and your hospitality." He stood from the table. The conversation was essentially over. "You don't have to worry about me," he said, hoping that it was enough to set her mind at ease about whatever it was she suspected of him. Because unless Meriam had tied the bedsheet around the woman from room one's neck and hung her from the latticework, Lance saw no threat in her. She was lying to him, that was for sure, but Lance got the sense that it wasn't out of self-preservation.

He felt like she was protecting somebody else.

"I'll be on my way in the morning," Lance said, heading for the door. "Thanks again for the coffee."

He waved and left her sitting there, alone with her secrets.

He went around the office's counter and pulled up his hood and cinched the strings tight and braced himself for the cold, which was just as fierce as he'd feared, and by the time he pushed through the door to room one and slammed it shut behind him, he was freezing again.

His room was dark, and as he was reaching along the wall for the light switch, he paused halfway. *The lights were on when I left. I'm sure of it.*

He found the switch and flipped it on and his head did something funny, like a temporary dizziness that danced around his skull. There was ringing in his ears, brief and quickly fading. His heart did a few rapid beats and caused his breath to hitch in his chest.

And then it all stopped and the lights came on and Lance was staring directly at the woman who'd killed herself.

[8]

BELIEVE IT OR NOT, IT WAS NOT THE SIGHT OF THE WOMAN in front of him—the woman who Lance knew was very much dead—that Lance's mind chose to focus on first. It was funny how the senses worked sometimes, the way the nose and ears and eyes could work together to unravel a mystery and discover oddities before a person even knew what was happening. But that was what was happening right now, because even though Lance was aware of the woman in his room with him, he was also much more aware that this *wasn't* his room.

Okay, that wasn't quite right. It was his room, but ... not exactly. He saw the same pictures hanging on the wall, but their frames were not milky with smudges and coated with dust. He saw the same two beds, but their wooden headboards shined and lacked the chips and pockmarks; the comforters were not forest green but a deep red that wasn't faded at all and looked like they might have just come from the packaging. The carpet was the same but looked fluffier, softer. Not worn down to the last few fibers from hundreds of sets of feet traipsing back and forth. The television was there, off now, and the beige plastic phone, looking more white than before. Lance inhaled, and any hint of mildew or unpleasant scents was not to be found. The room smelled fresh, like pine needles and leaves on the forest floor. His ears picked up voices, faint and laughing, from next door. The next room over. Was it a television or actual people? Either way, there were other people here, other people staying at the motel for the night. When had they arrived? How had he missed seeing their car in the parking lot as he'd walked from the office?

All these things collided in Lance's head, like the ingredients of a cake being dumped into a mixing bowl. Lance finally allowed his eyes to settle on the woman in front of him, the final ingredient, and when everything stirred together, he understood.

He was standing in his motel room, but he was not standing in the present. He was somehow seeing the past. And then a thought occurred to him and he reached out with one hand and pinched the skin on the back of his other hand, felt the sting and saw the crescent shapes left behind by his fingernails, and then he knew. It was impossible—there was that word again—but it was happening.

Lance wasn't just seeing the past. He was somehow a part of it.

Well, this is certainly a first. Guess I can add time traveler to my resume now.

He joked with himself, but at the same time there was a distinctive tremor of fear that passed through him. To stay focused, Lance chose to believe that whatever he was currently experiencing was just a more deeply manifested version of the dream he'd had earlier when he'd been standing in the road, staring at the copy-and-paste boy outside the motel. He didn't believe this, not really, but the bigger truth was too complex and too terrifying to contemplate at the moment.

The woman was sitting at the small table next to the bed,

the one where Lance had sat and charged his cell phone earlier —or was it several years later? He had no idea how to think about such things. It was one thing not to know where you were, but something completely foreign not to know *when* you were— and she was wearing a heavy green sweater and blue jeans. She'd kicked off her boots, which lay on their sides at the foot of the bed, and her feet were crossed at the ankles as she sat hunched over something on the table in front of her.

It was a sheet of paper, blank and waiting. The woman's right hand tap-tap-tapped an ink pen against the tabletop, her eyes staring down, just as blank as the page before her, lost deep in thought.

Lance took a small, tentative step forward. Wanted to see if his movement would cause any sort of reaction from the woman. It didn't, her eyes never leaving the blank sheet of paper. Which seemed so strange. To Lance, everything in and around the room, including the woman, was completely alive and real. This was more vivid and detailed and ... *exposed* than any dream or hallucination or vision could possibly be. This was literally reality, and it was as though Lance were the bit that wasn't real.

It's like I'm the dream, he thought, then shook his head. *No, it's like I'm the one on the other side, for once.*

Another tremble of fear. He didn't know what this thought might mean—but he briefly considered the idea that somehow he'd died, and even in death, the Universe refused to let him rest. Forced him to carry on as their soldier. And think about how much more productive he would be without all the distractions of being alive, like eating and sleeping and having to go to the bathroom.

He pushed these thoughts away. Took a breath to calm himself. And the fact that he felt himself inhale and exhale, felt the oxygen in his lungs and the beat of his heart in his chest, told him he was wrong. He wasn't dead. As usual, he chose to put his faith in the Universe and go along with things. *Business as usual, Lance. Go do your thing.*

As if he ever had any real idea what his thing was.

He took another step closer, a fuller stride this time, and then leaned down, slowly, peering at the sheet of paper, so close to the woman's face he could see the pores on her nose and fore-head, as well as the dark circles under her eyes she'd made a sloppy attempt to hide with concealer.

Lance remembered Meriam's story, how this woman had been searching for her lost child. She probably only slept when her body absolutely forced her, and even then the sleep was likely broken and full of who knew what kind of nightmares.

The sheet of paper was stationery from another hotel, a bigger chain, something the woman must have grabbed at a stop along her journey here. Same with the pen that had suddenly stopped tapping. The woman closed her eyes then, taking a deep breath, then another. When she reopened them, Lance saw they were wet with tears, a single drop beginning to fall down her right cheek. Then she put the pen to the paper and—

And when she started to write, the entire room began to wobble and the woman's actions sped up several times faster than her actual speed. Lance's vision jittered along with the ramp of speed, but he himself felt completely normal. He raised his hands in front of his face and wiggled his fingers and found his own movements to be regular speed. It was as if he were standing in front of an old VHS movie and somebody had pressed the fast-forward button on the remote.

He watched in high speed as the woman scribbled on the paper, stopping from time to time and sitting back in her chair and wiping her eyes or digging in her pocket to pull out a tissue to blow her nose. All this in the span of three or four seconds. A rapid succession of actions. Then the room came to a crashing halt, slamming back into regular life speed, and Lance watched as the woman folded the sheet of paper in half, then folded it again, a tight square. She wrote something on the outside of it, then set the pen down and sighed, using the backs of both her hands to wipe at her cheeks again. Lance leaned forward to read what she had written on the outside of the folded paper, but then the woman stood from the chair and somebody hit the fast-forward button again and the room *whooshed* back into overdrive and Lance took a staggering step back as everything around him began to jitter and jive again.

The woman fast-forwarded across the room to the alcove with the double sinks and flipped open her small suitcase she had on the counter. Reached inside and grabbed a handful of fabric. Zapped across the floor into the bathroom. Popped out a split second later wearing different clothes.

Oh no.

She was wearing flannel pajamas.

Lance watched in horror, rooted in place as the woman then rushed to the bed, flinging the comforter back and ripping off the sheet. Then she zipped back to the table and grabbed one of the chairs, only inches from Lance. He darted a hand out, lightning fast, hoping to grab her upper arm and stop her, but she passed right through, a small tingling in Lance's fingers. If the woman had felt him, her reaction had been impossible to see at such a speed.

And then in a flash she was beneath the wooden latticework, standing on the chair with the bedsheet tied above and the other end around her neck.

"No!" Lance yelled, but his voice sounded as if he were underwater, muffled and slowed and unintelligible, dampened by the jittering energy around him as the room speeded on. History speeded on, uncaring and uninterrupted by him, an out-of-place visitor.

Then the woman's mouth moved and she said something

Lance couldn't hear—maybe a goodbye to somebody unseen, maybe a message to her missing son—and then she shifted her weight and kicked the chair out from under her. Lance turned away, not wanting to see the fall, see the end result—he'd already seen it once.

And the room crashed back to normal again and Lance found himself looking directly at the sheet of folded paper on the table, and the word scrawled across the outside of it.

Meriam.

[9]

SHE'S LYING.

That was the thought that had flashed across Lance's mind when Meriam had told him she'd had no idea who the woman who'd killed herself was, or why she'd come to stay at the motel. Why she'd picked this very spot to end her life.

He'd had that thought then and he was having it again now. Meriam's name scribbled across the front of the dead woman's letter all but confirmed it. She knew more than she was letting on. She was holding secrets. Likely had been for many, many years. Ever since the woman had died.

But why?

Lance had to wonder how much if any of the story she'd told him—the woman coming from several states away to such an obscure location to look for her missing son—was true. But deep down, he felt there was some actual truth to Meriam's words, pieces of the puzzle that somehow fit together. But there were missing pieces, too. And Lance was going to have to find them.

The copy-and-paste boy, for one. That was a big piece, Lance knew. Who was he? What had he done? And, maybe most importantly, where was he now?

Lance reconsidered the words Meriam had uttered quietly from the cracked-open door when Lance had first arrived—*Is it really you?*—and thought about how taken aback she had had sounded. How full of wonder and disbelief and, yes, maybe even fear, her words had felt as they'd hit Lance's ears.

He's been gone a long time, Lance reasoned. *Why? And where did he go?*

The fact that Lance and the copy-and-paste boy bore a slight resemblance to each other, Lance was shelving away as nothing but a small coincidence.

But he could not fully shove away his mother's opinion on coincidences.

Do you, a person with your gifts, honestly believe things could be so random?

The motel room was still now, and as Lance continued to think and stare at the folded letter on the tabletop, the slight creaking of the wood as the dead woman's body swayed gently from where she hung was like a taunting playground bully. *Look at me, Lance*, it seemed to say. *Look what I had to do.*

Lance did not look. Instead, he decided to get answers, answers that had been sitting directly in front of him as he'd lost himself in contemplation. The letter beckoned to him, full of words that at the very least would give a direction to pursue. Ammunition to press Meriam harder to tell him the truth. He reached down to pick up the letter, but when his fingertips touched the paper, they simply passed through, first the letter and then the table. And then the room did another quick jitter and—

And he was standing back in *his* room. The photographs dusty again and the headboards chipped and tarnished and the carpet worn down. The pillows on the bed and the forest-green comforter showed his imprint from where he'd dozed earlier.

His cell phone charging cable snaked from the wall to the table where his flip phone sat charging.

No more letter.

He looked to his right.

No more dead woman.

He was back. Back from where, he still wasn't quite sure, but the sight of his cell phone made him quickly pick it up to check the screen. Still no service. A small, simple X where the reception bars should be. He couldn't say he was surprised. He set it back down on the table, gently this time so he wouldn't have to go chasing down another flying battery, and then he dashed around the bed and picked up the handset of the beige telephone. He pressed zero, waited three rings before Meriam picked up.

"Yes?"

"You're lying to me," Lance said, his adrenaline from the last few moments still pulsing through him, his frustration and confusion causing him to speak more harshly than he would have preferred. His mother would not have been impressed.

Meriam said, "I suppose I could say the same about you, don't you think?"

Lance said nothing. He'd been called out. But, *had* he lied? Or had he just omitted certain facts?

Was there really a difference?

He thought a moment longer, Meriam's breathing echoing across the line and into his ear. His only trump card would expose him. It wouldn't tell the whole truth of who he was, what his abilities were, but it would raise eyebrows and cause questions to be asked, and, to somebody in Meriam's position, potentially make him a curious threat.

How would she react? With swift capitulation and relief at being able to tell her story, a burden she'd been forced to carry all these years, just waiting for the right person to come along and offer her the moment of salvation she'd needed?

Or with anger, fast and hot and terrible?

In the end, Lance understood that he'd arrived at this motel for a reason—there was absolutely no denying that now—and he needed to do what he felt was right and deal with the consequences accordingly.

He just wished he could have had one more phone call with Leah first. He was beginning to understand that talking with her helped him think, offered fresh perspectives and advice and, well ... he missed her, what else could he really say?

"I know that the woman who killed herself wrote you a letter before she died. She left it on the table in this room. I'd like to know what it said."

Now it was Meriam's turn to go silent. A long pause in the conversation filled with a thousand unspoken questions. Finally, and Lance was relieved to hear not a denial, but an honest question, she said, "How could you possibly know that?"

Lance slowed himself down. He was pressing hard, for him, but this would still require some tactfulness to keep him from sounding like a complete lunatic. What could he say, really? *I watched her write it?* Instead, he said, "May I have another cup of coffee, and we can chat some more? I'm feeling a bit of insomnia coming on myself, I believe."

Meriam gave a soft sigh through the phone, and Lance imagined her, eyes closed, fist squeezed tight around the phone's handset, nodding her head, full of the realization that everything was finally coming to the surface. "Yes," was all she said, and then she hung up.

Lance replaced the handset onto its base and headed toward the door, then stopped himself. Glanced back at the phone. He felt silly for not thinking of it earlier, and while he knew Meriam would be waiting for him, the desire to make the call was stronger. He walked to his cell phone and pulled it from the charger, flipping it open and scrolling through his contacts until he found Leah's number. Then he walked back around the bed and picked up the plastic phone on the nightstand and dialed. Put the handset to his ear and waited.

Nothing.

No ringing, no busy signal, no beeping or tone or anything. Lance pressed the little plastic nub in the phone's cradle to end the call and start over. Dialed zero. The phone rang once and Meriam's voice answered, "Yes?" a bit impatiently.

"Yes, ma'am. I was just wondering, am I allowed to make outside calls from this phone."

"Of course," Meriam said, almost as if Lance had insulted her. But Lance thought there was some apprehension in her voice as well, as if she might be worried about who he might be calling.

"Right. Thank you. It's just, well, I just tried dialing a friend and nothing happened."

"Snow probably took the lines down. It happens from time to time. Welcome to rural America."

Lance nodded and said thank you again and assured her he was coming right over.

Right, he thought. *The snow. That's all it is.*

He replaced his cell phone on its charger and then pulled his hood over his head, cinching it tight and bracing for the cold. He walked to the door and reached out and grabbed the handle and turned it and two things happened at once: first, as soon as he began to turn the knob to open the door, he heard the faint sound of voices from outside, from near the room next door. Second, the room did another jitter, another *whoosh*, and then the door was open and Lance was staring out not at a parking lot full of snow and wind and the bitter cold, but at a warm, summer evening. The sky clear and with a pinkish-orange tint as the sun settled beyond the horizon, insects chirping and buzzing in the air, rock 'n' roll music playing from somewhere in the distance. A few cars in the parking lot, pulled in nose-first up to the doors of their owners' respective rooms.

Lance stared at all this, his mind desperately trying to catch up. He turned around, wanting to look back inside his room and see if it had changed as well, but as he did, he found he was already standing out on the walkway, unaware of having taken any actual steps of his own.

The door to his room was closed.

[10]

(1993)

Mark Backstrom's mother was finally gone, and as he drove his trusty blue Dodge pickup that he'd had since college down the rural road, balding tires rumbling over cracked asphalt, the summer sun finally setting after a long day of burning high and bright and hot, he thought to himself, *Good riddance to the bitch. Maybe now she'll finally let me be.* Then he looked over to his wife in the passenger seat and added, *Let* us *be.* It was the very first day of the rest of his and April's lives together. Alone. Finally.

Mark Backstrom's mother had been dead for two months.

It had been the longest sixty days of Mark's life. Because in death, his mother had become even more irritating than she'd been in life.

Elizabeth Backstrom's body had finally given in to her years of greasy foods, cigarettes, whiskey, and constant judgment. A small stroke, followed by a larger one two days later, had finally tamed the beast that had been a thorn in Mark's side his entire life, and a downright cannonball through the chest to April ever since Mark had announced that the two of them were engaged to be married.

"I've asked April to marry me, Ma," Mark had said, beaming, though sweating bullets inside, as he and April had sat at his mother's kitchen table, hand in hand, while Elizabeth lit a cigarette and fiddled with a pill bottle and seemed to try and occupy herself with anything except what her son was trying to tell her.

Her response had been simply to shake her head and stand from the table and say, "Oh nonsense. You'll come 'round. Now, who wants dinner? I've made lasagna."

April had cried the rest of the night. Mark had been furious. But he'd honestly expected nothing less from his mother, whose only happiness seemed to come from nicotine and alcohol and the misfortune of others. She'd been a miserable creature Mark's entire life, and even more so after Mark's father had died at the young age of fifty-two. A heart attack that adult Mark now liked to joke was his father's way of permanently escaping his mother's scornful look and sharp tongue. When Mark died—which he hoped would be roughly a hundred years from now—and if there was a Heaven where he might see his father again, Mark's very first question was going to be what could have possibly ever convinced him to marry Mark's mother. Mark could only assume the words *blackmail* and *shotgun* would be a part of the answer. Mark would even accept the phrase, *Well, your mother was pregnant with you, so...*

Though he hoped it wasn't that. Then he'd feel somewhat guilty for playing a part in sending his father to an early grave.

Despite his mother's disapproval, Mark and April did get married. No big wedding, just a simple trip to the courthouse with a few of their closest friends and April's parents. Mark had invited his mother the day before by calling her up on the telephone and letting her know the plans. Her response had been that she would not be missing *The Price is Right* to watch her only son make the biggest mistake of his life. Mark had said he understood—implying not that he agreed with the reasoning, but that he understood that she was a disgusting old hag who he honestly wished would just drop dead and be gone from his life.

Elizabeth acquiesced to this wish, but it took eleven years.

Well, eleven years and two months, to be precise.

Because while she'd been alive, her snakelike demeanor and insults and general displeasure at Mark and April's life could only be heard or seen via the telephone or the once-a-month visit for dinner Mark forced himself to have at his mother's house—which was a bit like a double-edged sword, because Elizabeth seemed to truly despise them being there, but also became incredibly insulted and derogatory when they failed to attend. But after she died ... she was everywhere.

Yes, when the hospital had called and delivered the news that his mother had passed away, Mark had breathed out a long-held sigh of relief, a breath of air full of a lifetime of frustration. April had shed a tear or two—which surprised Mark, given his mother's never-thawed coldness toward his wife—but the mourning period was brief, and only out of a sense of social obligation. But the relief was as brief as the mourning. Because Mark quickly discovered that while his mother's body was gone —incinerated to nothing but a pile of bone and ash and then buried in the earth and topped with a small gravestone—her effect on his life grew greater and more intimate than ever. In the worst possible way.

It had begun immediately after the burial, a small gathering at the back of the local cemetery that consisted of Mark and April, Elizabeth's remaining sister, Ginny—who was as startlingly pleasant and warm as her sister was heartless—and the minister from the Presbyterian church where Mark had not attended service in nearly a decade. After a few words were said and a few hugs were given and the remains of Elizabeth Backstrom were safely under the soil and out of everyone's sight and mind, Mark and April had walked back to the Dodge parked in the grass along the edge of the cemetery path and started the trip home.

The quickest way back to their single-story ranch house in the county was to jump on the highway and take a loop around the city and avoid the traffic. Mark had just taken the on-ramp and gotten the Dodge up to about sixty when he was suddenly overwhelmed by the sickening aroma of his mother's brand of cigarettes and her sour breath, reeking of whiskey and potato chips. And just as his mind registered the smell, his mother's voice came at him from over his shoulder, as if she were sitting in the nonexistent backseat.

"You always did drive too fast for your own good. It's a wonder I'm the one dead and you're still upright. Keep on like this and you'll be joining me soon." And to make matters worse, the words were followed by his mother's deep, phlegm-filled laughter that always graduated into a coughing fit that made it sound like her lungs were filled with pebbles and bubble wrap, as if the act of her breathing at all was a miracle that should be studied by doctors at some major university.

Mark had let out a yelp of surprise and spun around in his seat, nearly slamming the Dodge headfirst into the highway guardrail. If April hadn't taken the wheel and cried out, bringing Mark's attention back to the road, they both might have died. Which, Mark couldn't help but admit to himself, might have been his mother's intention.

Mark, too shaken up and too stupefied to even begin to think of a lie or excuse as to why he'd nearly driven himself and his wife to their deaths, parked the truck on the shoulder, and as cars whizzed by his window, he told April exactly what had happened.

When he was finished, she'd offered him a small smile full of sympathy and taken his hand. "Maybe your mother's death is hitting you harder than you want to admit. I mean, I know she was terrible"—she laughed, trying to lighten the mood—"but she was still your mother."

Mark nodded, and because he wasn't sure what else to say, he mumbled something that sounded like he agreed and then put the truck back into gear and waited for a break in traffic before stomping on the gas and driving the rest of the way home.

He didn't tell April that he still smelled the cigarettes and whiskey and potato chips.

After a restless but uneventful night's sleep, Mark was ready to convince himself that his episode in the Dodge was only due to stress, or maybe like April had said, it was some sort of delayed grieving that he wasn't aware he'd needed. He showered, dressed, and made his way to the kitchen, where April was sitting at the table in her pajamas, sipping a cup of coffee and reading the paper. She looked up and smiled at him, and he leaned down and kissed her on the mouth.

"Feeling better?" she asked.

"Yes, very much," he said, pulling a coffee mug from the cabinet and filling it. He turned back to the table to leaned against the counter. "I think yesterday I just—"

He dropped the mug, and it crashed to the floor and shattered to a million pieces, black coffee spreading across the linoleum like an oil slick on the ocean.

He hadn't even gotten the mug to his mouth for his first sip before the powerful, gag-inducing aroma of his mother hit his nostrils and he heard her whisper in his ear, "*Look at her, the lazy cow. Just sitting there while you get your own coffee. Can't even get up and pour you a bowl of cereal, if not cook you a real breakfast—eggs and bacon and all the things a growing boy needs. I always told you, Mark, you were always too good for that one. What a mistake you've made. What a sad, pathetic mistake."*

April was up in a flash, rushing to him and saying, "Baby, are you okay?" She was at his side, bare feet splashing through the spilled coffee, and Mark turned to her and said, "Can you smell her? Can you smell her? *Can you smell her?*" His eyes darted around, looking into the corners of the room as if at any moment his mother would materialize from hiding.

His heart was pounding in his chest, and April held him and stroked his hair and said over and over, "Shhh, it's okay. It's okay."

After he'd calmed down, his mother's scent having faded away, they cleaned up the kitchen, and he and April spent the rest of the day on the couch watching movies and late-night television and doing all they could to try not to talk about what had happened that morning in the kitchen.

But it didn't stop. It only got worse.

Mark's mother was everywhere.

At meals—*"The microwave again? A real woman knows how to cook for her man."*

At the barber—*"You're thinning out 'round the top, Mark. Might as well go ahead and tell him to buzz the whole thing for you. Better that way."*

At the advertising and public relations firm where Mark was a junior associate, desperately waiting for his chance to climb the ladder—*"Are you just going to sit there and let that old bag of dough talk to you like that, Mark? I didn't know I raised such a pussy."*

And worse still...

In the shower—*"Getting a little soft around the middle there, Mark. Might want to watch your sweets. Oh, and I guess you're a grower, not a shower."*

Mark's face had flushed redder than it had been from the steaming water, and he'd exited the shower stall so fast he'd slipped on the tile and nearly cracked his head on the edge of the toilet. He'd expected to hear his mother's hoarse laughter, but instead he'd only heard April's footsteps coming quickly down the hall and her asking loudly, "Mark, what was that? Are you okay?"

And then the bomb, the one that had sent Mark over the edge.

In his and April's bed, just on the heels of their lovemaking —*"It must be genetic. Your father used to make that exact same sound when he finished."*

"Go away!" Mark had yelled, bolting upright in the bed, April gasping and jumping up with him, their naked torsos glistening with sweat in the moonlight spilling through the window. "Go away, you bitch! You're dead! Leave me alone!"

After the panic had subsided and the anger flattened, Mark told April everything. Again. Just like he'd done in the Dodge that day after the funeral. Only this time, his wife's response had been to make him an appointment with a therapist and demand that he go. No excuses, no argument. Just a matter-of-fact thing he was going to do if she had to drag him there herself kicking and screaming the entire way.

Mark didn't hesitate. He couldn't spend the rest of his life with his mother breathing over his shoulder. He'd end up killing himself, which was terrifying, because then he might have to see her again if she'd managed to lie, cheat and steal her way into Heaven.

He went twice a week for two weeks to a lovely woman who smelled like mint and jasmine and spoke with a voice as soft and warm as a nice bath, a voice you could sink into and relax and lay down your worries. He told her everything without a shred of embarrassment, because if she had the answer to make it all stop, Mark would do whatever necessary.

They had great conversations, Mark and the woman who smelled of mint and jasmine, and she made some great points and said some very wise things about the effect a mother can have on her children, even in death. The experiences, for Mark, were cathartic and educational and overall very pleasant.

But also pointless.

Because his mother was right there, waiting for him after every single one of his sessions, just like she'd been when Mark'd been a child and had reemerged from the back of the dentist office to the waiting room or had come down the sidewalk to her waiting car on the days she'd picked him up from school.

"Learn anything useful today?" or *"So how much is she gouging you for?"* or *"You getting it on with her yet? I wouldn't blame you, considering the alternative at home."*

After the two weeks, Mark had called from work and canceled his next appointment. Told the receptionist he was going to look for another doctor to help him. She'd started to ask a question, but Mark hung up before she could finish.

He drove home, later that evening, trying to figure out how to tell April that he'd ended his therapy sessions, dreading having to tell her he'd failed, that his mother was still with him and he didn't know how to make it stop. Fearing as though he'd sound like a whiny little child who can't sleep without the lights on because he'll have nightmares about things that go bump in the night and live under the bed. He couldn't imagine a conversation that would make him—a grown man—sound less attractive to his wife.

But when he pulled into the driveway and parked and let himself in through the front door, he found April sitting at the kitchen table, an odd but somewhat excited look on her face.

"We're going to Pennsylvania," she'd said.

"Why?" That was all Mark could think to say.

"Because I think there's somebody there who can help you."

And so they'd come here to Pennsylvania, where they'd met him and it looked like everything might turn out alright.

The story was crazy, of course. The kind of thing that Mark would have ordinarily shaken his head and scoffed and wondered what sorts of people could be so gullible. But when he considered that he was effectively being haunted by the spirit of his dead mother—whether this was purely psychological or metaphysical or, yes, he was willing, at this point, to concede to the supernatural—Mark Backstrom was capable of accepting help in any form it might come.

"He called me on the telephone," April had said. "It was … the strangest conversation. And he knew it would be. He said, 'I know this is going to sound completely insane, and I can't explain it, but I know you and your husband are having some sort of trouble. I think something to do with a lost family member. I can help you, if you trust me.'"

Mark had been surprised to see that April's eyes had begun to tear up as she spoke.

"And I don't know how he knew, Mark, but when he talked to me, there was just something about it, something about his voice, or … I don't even know how to describe it, but it felt *right*. Almost like I was experiencing an answered prayer, live and in the flesh."

Mark knew then that April was serious. Neither of them had prayed in a long time.

Or maybe she had. Maybe in their newfound struggles, when no other option had seemed adequate, April had decided to pray for him behind his back. He wasn't sure if he should feel grateful or embarrassed or betrayed, but the look in his wife's eyes told him everything he needed to know.

She had an address scribbled on the back of a grocery store receipt—all that she'd been able to find at the time—and when she showed it to him, eyes full of hope and expectancy, Mark had pulled her close and kissed the top of her head and said, "Let's go."

Whether this person waiting for them would be the answer or not, Mark didn't want to spend another day in his home with his mother lingering over his shoulder. Thought maybe if he was going seventy on the interstate, they might be able to outrun her.

So now, with the truck tires rumbling and the motel coming into view up ahead, just before the bend, and not so much as a whisper from his mother or the faintest whiff of her cigarettes in hours, Mark Backstrom reached over and placed a hand on April's thigh and squeezed it.

"Thank you," he said.

She turned and smiled and placed her hand atop his. "Don't thank me," she said. "We can't thank *him* enough."

Mark still had no real idea how the young guy had made his mother vanish. They'd all simply had lunch together at a small diner in the town a few miles from the motel, with the guy sometimes lapsing into long moments of silence in their conversation, as if he'd become distracted by something none of them were bothered by. But for the hours they'd spent together after, as the boy had showed them around some of the local shops and then left them at the base of a short hiking trail he promised had some spectacular views, which Mark and April had hiked and laughed and embraced together, silently looking out across one of the gorgeous vantage points, and for the entire truck ride back, Mark's mother had been gone. Completely.

Mark thought about those moments of silence the boy had

drifted into. *That's when it was happening,* he reasoned. *I don't know what* it *was, but that's when he did whatever magic he needed to.*

Mark flipped on the Dodge's turn signal and slowed the truck enough to make the turn into the motel's parking lot. The place was well out of the way and not exactly a four-star (or even two-star) resort experience, but as far as he and April could tell so far, it was clean and quaint and quiet and maybe perfect, given the circumstances.

As Mark drove slowly to the front of their room, he saw the boy.

The boy was standing in front of their room, leaning against the exterior wall between their door and window and turning the pages of a *Superman* comic book. At the sound of the approaching truck, he looked up, and when he saw it was them, he smiled and waved and closed the comic book and looked completely at ease as he waited for them to park and exit the truck.

Mark and April walked up onto the walkway beneath the overhang and smiled back.

"Hey!" April said, running up and giving the boy a hug, "you were right about that trail. *Gorgeous.* We loved it."

"Good," the boy said, "I'm glad." Then he looked at Mark. "And you, sir? Did you enjoy yourself?"

Mark was no idiot. He heard the spoken words and all the unspoken meaning. He nodded his head. "I did. I truly did. Thank you so much. I don't think ... well, I don't think we would have ever found that trail without you."

The boy nodded, message received, the smile still big on his face.

Mark stuck out his hand, and the boy reached out and shook it, and while they were connected, Mark was hit with a desire so out of character for himself that he had to act before any thread of embarrassment could begin to poke through. He pulled the young man in close and wrapped his other arm around him in a friendly embrace. At the sight of this, Mark heard April give a soft sob of joy and then felt her body against them and her arms stretch around them and the three of them stood that way for a moment, silent and thankful.

When the boy left them with a farewell and safe travels and a friendly wave, disappearing into the motel's office, Mark looked at April, her eyes sparkling with happy tears, and felt such an unbridled, uninhibited sense of longing for her that he felt he could burst.

"Let's go inside," he said, giving her a sheepish grin.

April heard the spoken words and all the unspoken meaning.

They went into their room and closed the door.

Later, Mark Backstrom's ears picked up something that pulled him out of a dreamless sleep. His eyes opened and he peered into the near-darkness. Took a moment to remember where he was.

The boy. The motel. April…

He turned and found his wife beside him, a sheet draped over her naked body, her mouth opened slightly as she slept. He remembered the events from earlier, when they'd gotten back to the room, and smiled. It had been pure ecstasy, sex the likes of which they hadn't had since they'd been a new couple and had craved exploring each other's bodies.

Another noise, softer this time. His ears pricked up, and Mark squinted around the room, his vision still somewhat blurry from sleep. He shifted around and checked his wristwatch he'd placed on the nightstand, trying to use the faint glow of light coming in from the overhead lights outside the room to read it.

It was just after two in the morning.

He sighed and set the watch back down and rolled over to go back to sleep, and that was when he saw the shadow move out of the corner of his eye.

No, not a shadow moving, but something in the shadow coming forward, emerging from their hiding place in the corner by the door.

A figure clad in solid black, inching its way closer.

Mark cried out in surprise and scrambled for the lamp on the nightstand, nearly knocked it over before he found the switch and managed to get his fingers to work right and turn it on.

Harsh light assaulted the room, and Mark had to squint against the suddenness of it. April stirred beside him. "Mark?"

And then Mark's eyes adjusted and he saw the person standing at the foot of their bed. Black pants and shirt and a ski mask pulled down over their face.

A gun in their hand, pointed right at Mark.

LANCE STARED AT THE CLOSED DOOR TO HIS MOTEL ROOM for a long time. He'd known for sure that he'd not stepped across the threshold. He'd opened the door and had been prepared for the cold and was going to make his way to the motel's office to talk with Meriam, but instead of the snowstorm, he'd been greeted with a warm summer evening and voices, and before he'd had time to process it all he was on the sidewalk in front of the rooms, no memory of taking those couple steps, and certainly no recollection of closing the door behind him.

He reached out to grab the knob and—

"And you, sir? Did you enjoy yourself?" A voice. Male. Younger.

Lance swiveled in place, turning to his right and looking down the walkway to the room next door. A pickup truck had parked in front of room two, a dirty Dodge with the engine still hissing as it cooled. A small group of people standing in front of it, up on the sidewalk in front of the room's door, only a few feet from where Lance stood.

Lance felt himself surge with excitement. Or maybe it was a surge of relief, or better yet, thankfulness. Thankfulness for the fact that he might be about to get some answers, finally. Because one of the three people in front of room two, and presumably the owner of the voice Lance had just heard, was the copy-and-paste boy.

Up close for the first time, Lance saw that the boy was nearly as tall as he was, the frame long and wiry. His hair shaggy and unruly. He wore baggy clothes and had a comic book tucked under one arm. *Superman*, Lance thought he could read on the cover.

Yes, the resemblance was uncanny, in terms of build and physique, but as Lance looked at the boy's face, he again saw the differences. Above all else, the boy looked much younger than Lance. Maybe sixteen or seventeen. Face smooth and unblemished and not even a hint of stubble. He looked like a kid. But as Lance took a few small steps—tentatively, just like he'd done in his own room when the dead woman had been sitting at the table and Lance was unsure of his own effect on his new surroundings—moving around to get a better look at the boy, he looked into his eyes and he knew. Instantly he knew there was much more going on with the boy than what was present on the surface. He had the eyes of somebody much wiser than his years would suggest. Somebody who'd seen much more, experienced much more. It was a look Lance was familiar with, because it further reminded him of himself.

The other people on the sidewalk were a man and woman, middle-aged and husband and wife, Lance would guess, based on their respective wedding bands. The woman looked light and airy and full of ... was it hope, gratitude? The man's face was kind, but carrying something with it that hardened his features, as if he were still trying to work something out. But then, like the flip of a switch, his features softened and he answered the boy, "I did. I truly did. Thank you so much. I don't think ... well, I don't think we would have ever found that trail without you."

Lance watched as the boy nodded, a big smile of some deeper meaning and understanding forming across the boy's face. And then the man stuck out his hand for a handshake, which turned into a group hug, a tight embrace that somehow bonded the three of them. The woman was crying softly, but the tears seemed like those of somebody who was overwhelmed with happiness.

And then, as if his job was finished, the boy said, "It was very nice to meet you all. I'll leave you to enjoy the rest of your day. I'm glad you came."

"Oh, us too!" the woman said, giving the boy one last hug.

"Safe travels back home," the boy said as he turned to leave, giving them a wave. And then he walked right past Lance and started for the motel's office, leaving the man and woman alone on the sidewalk.

Lance gave another glance to the couple in front of room two, found them uninteresting as they stood together watching the boy leave them, and quickly turned back around to follow the boy.

The boy had just reached the door to the office and was pushing through it. Lance started quickly, wanting to catch up and not lose sight of the boy, unsure what would happen if he did. He still had no solid understanding of where or when he was, and what sort of rules applied to this new environment. He sprang to action and took two quick steps, sneakers pounding on the concrete, but then his entire being felt caught, snatched up and thrown backward in an exact reversal of his actions.

Like somebody had hit the rewind button on the remote.

The space around him had *whooshed* by in a blur and his legs had pumped in the opposite direction as before and he'd been spun around, and then everything went right back to normal and Lance was staring at the couple again, standing together on the sidewalk in front of room two as they watched the boy leave them.

Lance turned around in his spot, saw the same scene of the boy just reaching the motel's office's door and beginning to push through. Lance, out of sheer determination, tried to sprint even faster to catch up, to push through the door along with the boy.

Again. Two steps and the invisible bungee caught and snapped tight and pulled back and his peripheral vision danced and swirled and he was back where he started, looking at the middle-aged husband and wife, their faces reset in the exact same looks as before, staring after the boy as he made his way to the office.

Lance sighed. Looked over his shoulder and watched as the boy pushed through the office door and disappeared inside. When he was gone, Lance looked back to the couple and said, "Well, looks like it's just the three of us."

Point taken. This was where he was supposed to be. With them. He'd just have to wait and see why.

Neither the man or the woman heard or answered him. Lance was not surprised. He waited patiently.

The man looked to his wife, her eyes still wet with her happy tears, and said, "Let's go inside."

And Lance watched as the man and woman shared a look, one full of secret meaning that only they as a couple would understand. Unspoken words carried across by love. It made him think of Leah, and he wished he could be standing here with her right now. Looking into her eyes the way the man was looking into the woman's eyes. Hoping that she could understand all the things his look would tell her.

The man fished the room key from his pocket, same plastic key chain as the motel was using now—however far in the future Lance's now might be—and he unlocked the door and grabbed his wife's hand and pulled her in.

Lance moved as quickly—quicker, maybe—as he had when he'd tried to catch up with the boy, wanting to get inside the room before the couple closed the door on him. He had a flash of memory of reaching down to grab the letter the dead woman from room one had written Meriam, and how his hand had simply passed through it. If the man and woman closed the door to room two, Lance had no idea if he could open it—physically or mentally or in whatever state he existed in this new time and place. And he wasn't sure he was up to trying to pass through it, either, like Patrick Swayze in that movie *Ghost*.

Mom always liked that movie, Lance found himself thinking as he rushed to the door of room two. *Though she never watched the ending. Always said it was too sad.*

The couple disappeared into room two, and Lance took two more giant steps and then leapt through the shrinking opening as he saw the woman turn and begin to close the door—slowly, thankfully. He went airborne and headfirst, like a baseball player making a desperation slide for home plate, and for a moment he felt weightless, like he was breaking the laws of physics, but then he crashed down onto the carpet just as he heard the door click closed behind him.

He stayed that way for just a second or two, lying prone and facedown on the carpet, staring into the fibers and breathing in an aroma of dust mixed with the faintest hint of something akin to a more potent formulation of the baby shampoo his mother had used on him when he was just a little thing, laughing and splashing in the tub, probably the remnants of industrial carpet cleaner from long ago. He pushed himself quickly off the floor and stood, prepared to step out of the way of the man and the woman, wanting to become a fly on the wall for whatever might be about to transpire that the Universe had made sure he was going to stick around to see with his own eyes.

As he stood, a simple act that took him less than a second,

there was just a momentary flash in his vision as he made his way from prone to fully upright. But in that flash, everything changed.

The room was no longer gently kissed by the light of the setting sun creeping through the curtains. Instead, it was darkened, night having fallen. The small lamp on the bedside table cast a perimeter of harsh and artificial light that didn't stretch far and left the corners of the room dark and ominous.

The man and woman were dead.

The man's body was sprawled half on and half off the bed, near the end, his feet tangled in the bedsheets and his torso at a strange angle and his head resting sideways on the carpet, eyes open, mouth agape. He was naked except for his boxer shorts.

The woman was slumped back against the headboard, her naked torso rigid and stiff, arms splayed out at her sides like she'd gotten frustrated and given up and had fallen back in exhaustion. Her eyes were open as well, staring straight ahead toward the television as if she were absorbed in a show nobody else could see.

They both had bullet holes in their heads. The woman's was dead center of the forehead, execution-like. The man had one here as well, but as Lance leaned down to look more closely, he saw that the guy had also taken another shot, this one high up on the right side of his chest. Blood had spilled down the man's rib cage and dried in a darkened smear. Lance tried to put the pieces together in his head, imagine what had happened. Figured the man had tried to take down the intruder, taken him by surprise maybe, thus the impromptu and poorly placed shot to the chest. Then the killer had performed the kill shot to the head. More precise. Planned for.

The woman, probably stunned in terror at witnessing her husband's murder, hadn't even had time to react fully before she'd suffered the same fate.

Lance recalled the image of the two of them out on the sidewalk together, that look they'd shared, silent but tremendously loud all the same. So much love. He hoped they were together somewhere else.

And then Lance noticed something shift in his peripheral vision, slow and quiet. He'd still been crouched on the floor by the dead man's body, and from the corner of his eye, he saw movement on the bed.

Lance Brody lifted his head and looked to the woman.

She was sitting up now, her back ramrod straight, arms still dangling limply at her sides, palms up. The light from the lamp on the bedside table cast her huge shadow against the wall, like an image from a long-ago monster movie. Her neck twisted toward Lance, and her dead eyes fell on him and her mouth opened and she said, *"He'll be waiting."*

[12]

"*He'll be waiting.*"

Those words again. The same three words uttered by the dead woman from room one as her hanged body had dangled from the bedsheet she'd used to kill herself. Lifeless, but able to reanimate just long enough to deliver the message.

The same as the woman on the bed now in room two. A bullet hole through her forehead, body limp, but her blank stare able to find Lance and her words able to reach his ears, his mind.

What did it mean? *He'll be waiting.* Who? Where? When?

The usual gamut of curiosity cascaded through Lance's thoughts. This was twice now he'd been given the same information from two different ... what were they exactly? Lance had spoken to enough spirits, ghosts, lingering dead, whatever you wanted to label them, to understand that the women in room one and two were something different. They were not as *alive* as ghosts were—for lack of a better term. There was no interaction between them and Lance. They were more like envelopes, sealed long ago by the past, waiting for somebody to come along so they could open themselves and reveal their contents.

Waiting for Lance.

And now, apparently, somebody else was waiting for Lance, too.

"Who?" Lance asked, his own voice surprising him. It sounded strange, off-kilter. Distorted in some way, yet only just noticeable. It was flat, the echo and reverb you'd expect to hear in the enclosed environment of the motel room somehow eliminated, as if his voice had been run through some elaborate piece of audio processing software.

Because I'm not really here, Lance thought. Wherever *here* was, the past or some cosmic recreation of it, Lance's presence here was created in some other time and space. He existed here, but only on a certain level. And he had no idea what limitations that level held him to.

"Who will be waiting?" Lance tried again.

The dead woman with the bullet hole in her head did not move for a moment, her empty eyes locked onto Lance for another few seconds before her neck twisted back to its normal position, gaze fixed straight ahead, back onto the blank television screen. Then her entire torso inched its way backward, arching down slowly toward the headboard. Her bare back came to rest half on the pillow, half on the wood of the headboard, and then she was again completely motionless, having stopped in the exact same position she'd been in when Lance had first seen her.

The position she'd been in when she'd been murdered.

Lance stood still for a full minute, waiting to see if the woman would repeat her movements and message, like some sort of animatronic character at Disney World. But she did not. Lance sighed and looked down to the man and—

And the man was gone, a dark wet spot on the carpet where the blood from his chest wound had pooled the only evidence he'd been there at all. Lance took a quick step backward and then looked back toward the woman.

She was gone, too.

In the blink of his eyes, and in the slightest shifts in Lance's line of vision, the world around him seemed to be able to change and morph and speed up and slow down however it chose to. It was moments like these when Lance felt helpless. Completely at the mercy of whatever guiding force was running the show.

But the moments also gave a sense of encouragement. It was as though his hand was being held and he led along the proper path, being shown only what he needed to see and cutting out all the unnecessary bits. It was a path with a purpose.

But that didn't mean Lance had any better understanding what that purpose was.

Or who it was that was waiting for him.

Lance looked down again at the puddle of blood seeping into the motel room's carpet. Something was different about it. No ... not about the blood, or the carpet, but...

The bed. The bed was different. Lance let his eyes slide from the headboard all the way down to the end, where the man had been lying tangled in the comforter and—

The comforter is gone, Lance realized. On the bed now there was nothing but the plain white sheets, pulled back and twisted, splattered faintly with a spray of blood near the end where the man had probably first been shot.

Outside, the sound of an engine cranking to a start sounded like an explosion after the motel room being so still and quiet. Lance spun around and rushed to the window to peer through the blinds. He reached up with one hand, fingers splayed to pull down the slats to look through, and his hand went right through, a very faint tingling spreading through his fingertips when it did. Lance pulled his hand back and clutched it to his chest, then opened and closed his fist, testing to make sure everything was still in working order. Everything seemed fine.

The engine outside the room had been idling, and Lance's

ears picked up a change in frequency as the vehicle was shifted into gear.

I've got to get out of here, Lance thought. Because everything about the moment told Lance he needed to see what vehicle that engine noise belonged to, and hopefully who was driving it.

He looked at the motel room door. Studied it for longer than he felt he had time for. Remembered the tingling in his fingers as he'd passed through the blinds and wondered what that would be like if it spread across his entire body. Thought about Patrick Swayze in *Ghost* again and then wondered how many people had gotten injured or killed attempting to do something they'd seen in the movies.

Fiction versus reality.

Lance Brody lived somewhere in the middle.

He ran for the door. Whatever was going to happen, he'd rather it happen fast.

Four quick steps and he was there, charging straight for it. It went against everything instinctive about being a human, having your brain convince your body to continue full-speed and hurl itself into a solid object. Lance squeezed his eyes shut on the last step, felt his face pull back into a grimace, prepared for impact, and then he threw up his arms in front of his body and pushed through the final step and instead of a painful collision he felt ... almost nothing at all. Almost as if he himself were nothing at all. Weightless, floating, empty.

And then he felt concrete under his sneakers instead of carpet, smelled the sticky summer night air, and heard the sounds of the engine growling and tires purring directly in front of him.

It was the blue Dodge pickup the man and woman had arrived in. The headlights were off and Lance had made it outside the room just in time to watch as the unseen driver finished off a three-point turn and then drove forward across the parking lot, picking up speed as they approached the road.

Lance sprinted after the truck, finding himself halfway across the parking lot before he even knew he was moving. He wanted to try and get a glimpse of the driver, but he knew that in the darkness of night and given the fact he was so far behind, it would be impossible. But he'd seen something else as the truck had finished its maneuver in the parking lot before heading off.

A piece of heavy red fabric poking out of the tailgate where it'd gotten caught. Probably when somebody had closed it in a hurry and hadn't been paying attention, distracted by the task at hand. Lance knew it was the comforter from the motel room bed. And he knew exactly why it was in the back of the truck.

It was covering the dead bodies of the man and the woman. Their murderer was stealing their truck and disposing of them. Which caused Lance to have a thought: the murder must have been premeditated. Somebody doing a smash-and-grab job, a robbery gone wrong, maybe, would have left the bodies behind and fled the scene with no questions asked. No, there was more at work here. This had been planned.

The truck slowed just a bit to make the turn onto the road, and Lance saw his chance. He changed his path and started moving on a diagonal, pumping his legs hard to pick up speed just as the truck's front tires hit the road. If Lance was fast enough, he could essentially cut it off and be positioned perfectly to see the driver's face as the truck passed him by.

Or you could jump in front of it. See if they'll stop.

This was a thought meant for Lance in the present, not this past world he was currently trapped in. He remembered that the driver of the truck wouldn't be able to see him at all, and even though Lance's body seemed to be able to pass through objects, convincing himself to jump through a closed door was one thing, hoping a speeding pickup truck would simply pass through him and leave him unharmed was quite another.

He cried out with the effort of his sprint, saw the truck encroaching in on him in his peripheral vision. Three more steps and he could jump out into the road, just where the end of the motel's parking lot met the shoulder and the truck would just be passing.

One and two and three and as his sneakers left the parking lot and were about to land on road, the entire world spun around and Lance felt that weightless feeling from earlier when he'd passed through the door, coupled with a great sense of speed, and when his sneakers found the ground again he was standing right back where he'd started as the truck had been pulling away, right back in front of the door to room two.

In the distance, far off to his left, he heard the growl of the Dodge's engine fade away to nothing, leaving Lance standing alone on the sidewalk, chest heaving as he fought to catch his breath. Thirty seconds, maybe a minute, and his breathing returned to normal, but his curiosity had not waned at all. With his eyes locked onto the spot across the parking lot where he'd felt the Universe grab him and hurl him back to his starting point, Lance stepped off the walkway and started walking.

He stopped just short of where the parking lot ended and the road began, his eyes searching in the darkness for anything out of the ordinary, anything to signify that this spot was different, or held some sort of energy.

Lance saw nothing.

He shrugged, figured he'd survived enough of these moments not to have to worry too much, and then took the last step, crossing the threshold of the parking lot.

Again, before his sneakers hit the ground, he was back in front of room two, his vision just clearing from the crazy, unexplainable trip. Another blur of sound and light and the great rush of speed.

He started walking again. This time in a straight line across the parking lot, right up the middle, stopping right at the road. He stood and looked across the blacktop, saw the dancing of fireflies in the air, swirling among the high grass and the trees. He looked left and right, saw no traffic, and then stepped out onto the road.

And was right back in front of room two.

Which, of course, confirmed it. Lance remembered when he had first arrived at the motel, the way he had somehow blacked out and then woken up on the snow-covered ground. It had happened right as he'd crossed the threshold, leaving the road and entering the parking lot.

Some sort of barrier, Lance thought. *A dividing line between the rest of the world and whatever this is.*

But the thought that followed this was much more sinister.

Whatever force governed this barrier had let Lance in, but it didn't want to let him leave.

Not until I'm finished, he thought. *Whatever that means.*

Movement caught Lance's eye, and he swung his head to the right in time to see the door to the motel's office swing shut behind somebody who'd just stepped inside.

Somebody else had been out here when the truck had pulled away.

Somebody else had been watching.

Somebody else knew exactly what had happened.

[13]

Lance hurried to the door to the motel's office and stopped outside of it. Peered in through the glass and saw nobody inside, just the same layout—the check-in counter, the ledger book, the bowl of peppermint candies, and the watercooler, though it was an older model than what had been there when Lance had checked in earlier ... or later, rather, if he was still seeing the past. But the door to the back living area where Lance had shared coffee with Meriam was wide open and the lights were on, so somebody had to be back there. Somebody had just come through the door, and unless they were hiding in the darkened bathroom at the rear of the office, there was nowhere else they could be.

Much like his second test run against the barrier at the edge of the motel's parking lot, Lance didn't hesitate this time. He just closed his eyes and took a deep breath and walked through the office door.

He felt the floor give way beneath his sneakers and felt the tug at his gut and then the brief sensation of being everywhere and nowhere all at once, a roller-coaster moment where he wasn't sure which way was up or down, and then just as quickly as it had started, everything settled back to normal and he felt the rubber of his shoes touch down on the floor and—

"You're doing it again, aren't you?"

Lance opened his eyes and saw not the empty motel office he'd seen through the door just a moment ago, but instead two people standing on opposite sides of the L-shaped check-in counter. The room was much brighter than before, and Lance quickly turned around in his spot and looked outside. Gone was the night sky, and instead intense sunlight poured through the door's glass. A hot summer day was nearing its end, the sun settling itself into position before it would start its descent. In the window next to him, the blinds were pulled down and sunlight slid through the cracks in the slats, giving the floor and part of the check-in counter a prison-cell effect. Curious, Lance stuck his hand out into the rays of light, turning it this way and that. The light passed right through, as if Lance weren't there at all.

He'd never felt more like a ghost.

"Doing what?"

Lance focused his attention back to the people at the counter.

A version of Meriam that looked maybe twenty years younger, wearing cut-off shorts and a faded flannel shirt with the sleeves rolled up to her elbows, stood behind the counter with her hands on her hips, her head cocked to the side. Her hair was darker and fuller, her body more lively and fit.

She rolled her eyes and said, "Don't play dumb with me. We both know you're too smart for that."

The copy-and-paste boy was on the other side of the counter, leaning down, resting his elbows on the surface top, flipping the pages of a comic book he had laid out before him.

Superman, Lance thought. And then he saw the boy was wearing the same clothes he'd been wearing when Lance had seen him talking with the man and woman who'd been murdered in room two. Which suggested a couple different possibilities: either the boy just happened to be wearing the same clothes in two different of these episodes Lance was experiencing, or Lance was seeing events from the exact same day as before, only earlier. The *Superman* comic caused Lance to lean toward the latter.

His mother had not been a believer in coincidences, after all.

"Look at me," Meriam said, this time with a no-nonsense tone.

The boy looked up, then stood to his full height, towering over the counter just as Lance did. Lance took two steps closer, stopping just shy of the boy.

"Are you doing it again?"

They were both quiet for a moment, and Lance could practically hear the gears turning in the boy's head as he struggled with some sort of internal debate—a conflict in which he wasn't quite sure which direction to take. Finally, he let out an exasperated sigh and nodded his head.

Meriam, apparently displeased by this response, looked down to the floor and put both her hands on her head and shook it slowly back and forth. "You don't even know these people."

"Are we only supposed to help people we know? That doesn't seem very Christian of you."

Lance chuckled at this, but Meriam looked up with fire in her eyes. "I know you aren't questioning what kind of person I am, young man. Not after all I've ... well"—she paused, looked around the office as if somebody else might be listening—"not after everything."

The boy shook his head, sighed again. "Of course not. I'm just showing you how I see it. These people need help, and I can give it to them."

"By exposing yourself? Is that really the best choice?"

The boy thought for a moment, then smiled a smile that Lance thought might be hiding a certain degree of sadness. "The fact that you think I have a choice at all makes me think you really have no idea what it's like to be me."

Meriam didn't like this either, Lance could tell, but her features softened a little and she stepped forward and placed her hands on the countertop. "If you're asking me if I can empathize with somebody who has your ... what do we want to call them, gifts or talents? Then, no, I can't. And honestly, who could?"

Lance was at once enthralled by the conversation. Maybe more so than any conversation he'd ever listened in on throughout his entire life—with either the living *or* the dead. Because what he was hearing was a conversation he himself had been a part of many times over, both with his mother and with himself and with Marcus Johnston and even somewhat with Leah. Not the exact same words or the exact same situation, but the context was there. Nearly unmistakable. Between the exchange Lance was hearing now and all of the evidence he'd witnessed in his wild ride around the motel's history lesson, it had to be so.

The copy-and-paste boy, to some extent, was like Lance. In some capacity, he possessed otherworldly—

"Abilities," the boy said.

"What?" Meriam asked.

"These things I can do, I would never call them gifts. And neither would anybody who truly understood what it was like to live with them."

Meriam was quiet then, her gaze shifting into something that looked stuck between sympathy and frustration. The boy said, "Look, you know I love you, and of course I appreciate all you've done for me over the years, but you have to understand this is just who I am. I didn't ask for it, but that doesn't change anything. Why else would I have been chosen by whatever power decided to make me this way if I wasn't supposed to use these abilities to their fullest extent? It's my *duty* to help these people. Don't you understand that?"

"I do!" Meriam threw up her hands. "But don't you *worry*? Aren't you concerned that if the wrong people discover who you are, things could go terribly wrong terribly fast? I'm no scientist or theologian or anything special. I'm just a simple woman who runs a country motel. But even I have the common sense to think that if there's a *power*, as you put it, that made you who you are, there's a good chance there's an opposite power that wants to put an end to you."

She's a lot smarter than she gives herself credit for, Lance thought, wishing he could get back to the present to have his conversation with her. Especially after having gathered all this additional information about who he was dealing with. Meriam had already known one person in her life who was like Lance, and Lance thought she was sharp enough to recognize him for what he was. In fact, she likely already had.

Lance noticed the silence in the room. Looked and saw that the boy's head had dropped back down to the comic book on the countertop. And Lance saw some great secret there. Something hiding behind the boy's kind eyes.

He knows something, Lance thought. *He knows she's not wrong.*

The boy looked back to Meriam. "I can't live in fear," he said. "None of us should."

"But you can be *cautious*," Meriam countered.

The boy shrugged. "Some people don't know the difference."

Meriam didn't disagree with this but added, "Just remember what happened with that woman who hanged herself in that room right over there." Meriam pointed to the far wall, to room one. "Remember the effect your *helping* can have on others. Remember *us*."

"That's not fair," the boy said. "I knew she was grieving, but despite my abilities, I can't predict the—"

"*Exactly*. You don't know everything. And I might not have all of your *abilities*, but I've got enough common sense to know you can't just go around trusting everyone."

"I don't disagree with that," the boy said calmly.

"Then what is it you're not telling me?"

The boy said nothing. Lance waited.

"Well?" Meriam said. "You agree, at least by omission, that there *could* be people out there who, let's say, don't have your best interests at heart. And believe me, I'm showing a lot of restraint by phrasing it like that. And you also agree that, despite your good intentions and obligation to help people, you simply can't live your life trusting everybody you meet. Do I have that right?"

The boy nodded. "Yes."

"You see the dilemma here, right? Your thinking doesn't match up with your actions. What is it I'm missing? These people today, the..." Meriam pulled the registration book over and slid her finger down the list of names until she found what she was looking for. "The Backstroms. How are you so confident that when you're finished helping them, there won't be repercussions, or hidden agendas, or, I don't know, three years from now, one of them says something to somebody else about what you did for them and that sets off a chain of events that leads to you being abducted by some government agency? Snatched in the middle of the night with a black bag thrown over your head and jetted across the country to some top-secret facility where they'll make you nothing more than a test subject in an effort to figure out how they might be able to weaponize *whatever* the hell it is you have?"

"That's oddly specific."

Meriam slammed her hand on the countertop, the noise echoing like a gunshot in the office. "I'm serious, dammit!"

And then there was silence again. Lance stood and watched, his heart beating fast in his chest as he'd gotten caught up in the drama unfolding back and forth between the two people in front of him. He was experiencing the oddest form of elation, a sense of belonging unlike anything he'd ever felt before. For the first time in Lance's life, he was standing in the presence of somebody else who knew exactly what it was like to be him. Somebody who understood the toll it took on the mind. Somebody who had to fight the frustrations of being unable to explain the full truth to somebody who wasn't like them. Which, up until this moment for Lance, had been every other human being he'd ever met. Unfortunately, as of now, the other person who Lance wanted so desperately to meet and speak with, was nothing more than a figment from the past.

As if on cue, the boy began to move, walking around behind the counter, where he reached out and embraced Meriam, his long arms wrapping around her and pulling her close. "I can't explain it," the boy said softly.

Meriam said nothing for a moment, and then, as she gently pulled away from the boy's embrace, she asked, "Can't or won't?"

The boy smiled. "Just trust me, the Backstroms will not be the end of me."

Which Meriam picked up for the omission it was. She countered, "You would tell me if you knew something else, right? You would tell me if you thought something bad was going to happen? You would let us help you, right?"

The boy smiled again, and again Lance saw something

hiding behind those eyes. Saw a tall, good-looking young man with an outward easy-going persona, a bashful sense of innocence. A young man who, under normal circumstances, should have an entire world to explore, an entire life to go and live to its fullest. But, Lance knew, inside the boy harbored secrets he could tell no one, carried with him a soul riddled with guilt and regret, found himself drowning in confusion so deep he thought he'd never see the surface again. Never take another breath of normal life. He was alive, but often wondered if he was living.

Lance saw himself.

"Of course I'd tell you," the boy said.

And Lance knew he was lying. He'd had to tell similar lies himself.

You told the lies to protect others as much as you did to protect yourself.

Meriam said nothing for a long time, just stood back and looked up into the eyes of the young man who towered over her, searching for hidden meaning, pleading for the truth. *Because she knows*, Lance thought. Meriam knew the boy held secrets, understood that there were deeper truths locked away inside him that he very well might take with him to his grave. At the core of her, she knew these things, but Lance also saw the reluctance on her face, watched as the easier option presented itself to her.

She would have to trust the boy. She would have to accept the fact that whatever he wasn't telling her was absolutely for her own good. Lance's own mother had made her peace with this unfair side of their relationship very early in Lance's life. She'd never prodded, never guilted him into divulging information he wasn't ready to tell. But she could always sense when something was amiss, always had that motherly instinct that was triggered every time her son was wresting with something in his mind, unsure, lost, afraid, desperate to escape the burdens he'd been born with.

Meriam nodded, forced a smile and then reached up and patted the boy's cheek. "Good," she said. "You know we're always here for you."

The boy reached up and took her hand in his and kissed it. "Hey, where is Uncle Murry, anyway?"

Meriam began to busy herself with some pamphlets on the countertop. "Oh, he went fishing with Jimmy and Drew. Never mind the fact we got shingles need replacing and room six's showerhead is leaking." Meriam sighed but then followed it with a laugh. "What am I ever going to do with him?"

The boy walked back around the counter and scooped up his comic book. "Oh, I'm sure you'll think of something. I can help with the shingles tomorrow, maybe."

Meriam shook her head. "Nope. No way I'm sending you up on that roof. If anybody's going to fall off it or through it, it's going to be *him*."

The two of them shared a laugh, and Lance stepped out of the way as the boy headed for the door. "I think they're almost back. I want to check in with them and see how things went."

Before the boy could leave, Meriam asked, "How bad was it?"

The boy stopped. Looked over his shoulder and said, "What?"

"For the Backstroms. How bad was whatever it was you had to help them with?"

The boy thought for a moment. "Nothing as tragic as the woman from room one, but ... I think it had the potential to ruin their lives. At least their marriage. And they're really good people, Aunt Meriam. They deserved to be happy together. I think that's why I picked up they were having trouble."

Lance was very curious about the boy's phrasing: *I think that's why I picked up they were having trouble.*

Picked up.

He badly wanted to ask the boy what that meant. Wanted to compare their abilities and intuitions and ... *everything.*

Meriam nodded and then pulled a bottle of Pledge from under the counter and started spraying down the countertop. "Stop back in before you head home for the day. Maybe Murry will have some fish you can take home."

The boy nodded. "Yes, ma'am." And then he pulled open the door and stepped outside.

Lance didn't hesitate. He moved fast and furious, not wanting to let the boy out of his sight. He didn't even pause to take a deep breath and prepare his body for another moment of ... what, transformation? Teleportation? Another Swayze moment? He didn't have time to contemplate a proper label of the phenomenon. Hell, this entire day had been a phenomenon. He rushed across the floor and threw his body into the door leading outside.

The feeling of speed. The rushing of everything, as if he was suddenly not existing in any time or space and then being rapidly reassembled whole. Another crash landing of sneakers on—

Lance was not outside. Not on the sidewalk with the summer sun setting and the copy-and-paste boy heading down the sidewalk to lean against the motel's wall, comic book opened in his hands as he waited for the Backstroms to return.

Lance was back in the office. Dim and full of shadows. He spun around, finding nighttime had returned. But what night was it? How could he ever know?

Voices. Coming from behind him. Lance turned back around and saw the bar of light slicing through the cracked door behind the check-in counter. The door to the living space where

Meriam and, presumably, Murry lived together as they ran their business.

"Calm down," a male voice said. Deep and borderline authoritative, but also concerned. "Meriam, take a breath, for God's sake."

"They're going to come for him! I told him, Murry. I told him this would happen. Just today I did, but he wouldn't listen."

"*Stop!*" Murry's voiced boomed through the crack between door and frame. "You're overreacting. Just because you think—"

"I *heard* them. They said—"

"People talk, Meriam. People talk all the time. They very rarely do anything."

Meriam scoffed. "You sound like him."

"And what exactly does he think about this situation? Have you told *him*?"

Lance started moving, heading around the counter to try and get a look inside the room.

"We got in a bit of tiff earlier about this sort of thing," Meriam said.

"And?"

Meriam sighed. "And he's not concerned, *okay*? But when is he ever, huh? I don't think he fully understands the way the world works."

Murry actually laughed at this. "I would argue he knows more about the way the world works than you or I ever will."

Lance reached the door and positioned his face so that one eye could peer through the opening. He didn't want to try and move himself through it, because he wasn't sure he'd actually end up where he thought he was supposed to. To say that at this point he felt out of control of his entire situation would be the understatement of his life.

Murry was a short man, only a couple inches taller than his wife. Slim but wired with ropey muscle on display beneath his t-shirt. His blue jeans were spotted with dirt, as were the work boots he wore on his feet. His hair was buzzed close to his scalp. Stubble peppered his face. He reminded Lance a bit of Leah's father, Sam, only with kinder eyes.

"But that doesn't mean he's always right, Murry," Meriam said, her voice pleading. When Murry said nothing, Meriam added, "He's like our son, Murry. *Our son.* It's our job to protect him. And we owe it to my sister."

Now it was Murry's turn to scoff. "Hardly."

"The only reason we have this place is because of her. You know that."

Murry said nothing. Lance desperately tried to keep up, tried to make sense of the conversation.

Finally, Murry threw up his hands, an act of capitulation. "What exactly is it you'd like me to do? I can't force them never to talk about any of this."

Meriam nodded. "I know, I know. But maybe..." Then she moved out of sight, headed toward where the sofa had been when Lance had been inside the room with her in the present. Murry stayed where he was, arms crossed, watching his wife. Waiting.

Minutes passed by. Lance didn't move, afraid that if he looked away, the entire scene would change and he'd end up in some other place, some other time. Finally, Meriam's voice disturbed the silence.

"I have an idea," she said.

And then the sound of a bell giving off its *ring-a-ding* echoed in the empty office space behind Lance, and he turned around so fast his entire vision blurred and danced and he felt so dizzy he thought he might vomit and—

And then everything slowed and returned to normal. Except...

Except it was no longer nighttime. And he was no longer alone in the office.

The room was a muted gold as early-morning light warmed the space. Murry was hunched over the check-in counter, wearing clean blue jeans and a t-shirt, though the work boots were still spoiled with dirt. He had a cup of coffee on the countertop next to him, beside a plate of bacon and what looked like the remnants of scrambled eggs. A newspaper was splayed out beside this, turned to the sports section.

But Murry wasn't looking at the newspaper. His eyes were turned upward toward the person who'd just walked through the motel office's door. It was a young girl, dressed in checked pajama pants and mismatched neon-colored socks. A baggy sweatshirt fell nearly to her knees. Her hair was tangled from sleep, but her eyes said she was very much awake.

Lance recognized her immediately as the girl he'd seen from his vision earlier when he'd watched the copy-and-paste boy embrace the fuzzy-television people outside the motel rooms. The girl who'd been in front of room five. Though up close now, Lance thought his early guess at her age might have been off. Now, standing in front of him, with her features more prominent, Lance thought she might be thirteen or fourteen. Older than he'd initially thought.

She walked up to the counter in her socked feet. Murry stood up straight and smiled. "Yes, ma'am, can I help you?"

Lance could hear the concern in his voice.

The girl said, "My dad is dead."

(1993)

Alexa Shifflett was at her friend Maggie's house when the press conference started. They were on the floor in front of the couch in Maggie's living room, legs stretched out in front of them and bowls of popcorn balanced precariously on their thighs as they watched Nickelodeon on cable and tried to secretly put popcorn in each other's hair.

"Have you seen *Jurassic Park* yet?" Maggie asked with a mouthful.

Alexa shook her head, took a sip of Pepsi from the can beside her. Her dad never let her have drinks in their own living room, telling her he didn't want her to spill them and stain the carpet or the couch. Her dad was always worried about things like that. Their house was always super neat and tidy, and when people came over, they always jokingly asked, "Geez, does anybody even live here?"

Alexa's dad would laugh along with them, but Alexa could tell he was secretly pleased. And Alexa felt a bit of pride at this, too, because her daily chore list was one of the reasons the house always looked the way it did—what with her vacuuming and dusting and doing the dishes (always drying them and putting them away, because dishes left in the drying rack were an eyesore!).

Alexa had always assumed her dad's fastidious habits of neatness and cleanliness had something inherently to do with him being a police officer, because in all the movies about war and soldiers, you always saw the parts where the soldiers were told to make their beds real neat and shine their shoes real nice and somebody was always screaming in their face if they didn't. Actually, somebody was usually screaming in their face even if they did what they were told. She knew that being a soldier and being a police officer were two different things, but the correlation still made sense to her twelve-year-old self.

"No," Alexa said. "Haven't seen it yet. Daddy's supposed to take me soon, but he's been *really* busy at work lately. I can't wait, though. It looks *soooo* scary."

Maggie washed her mouthful of popcorn down with her own sip of Pepsi. Burped and then said, "It is! We went two nights ago and mom nearly ripped my dad's arm off. Dad said he's going to have a bruise for weeks! My favorite part is when the T. rex—"

Alexa shot a hand out and pressed her palm against Maggie's lips, Maggie's eyes going wide in surprise. "Hey!" Alexa said, "Don't ruin it for me, dork!"

Maggie started to lick the palm of Alexa's hand and Alexa shouted, "Ewwww, gross!" and wiped her hand on the side of Maggie's face. Which then prompted Maggie to take a handful of popcorn and try to stuff it down the front of Alexa's shirt, which led to a bit of a wrestling match in which, surprisingly to everyone, not one Pepsi can ended up sideways.

"Okay, okay, enough, girls," Maggie's mom, Trish, called out as she entered the living room. She was rushing across the carpet to the television. "I swear, you two can be more like boys than girls sometimes." She started pressing buttons on the front of the television, changing the channel up, up, up. "Oh for goodness' sake, Mags, what channel is—"

"Mom, like, you can use the remote, you know? Technology is a good thing!" Maggie said, rolling her eyes at her mother, causing both her and Alexa to burst out laughing.

"Oh, here it is. *Shhhhh*, girls, please."

Something in Trish's tone set both the girls straight immediately, and when Alexa's eyes locked on to what was being shown on the TV screen, suddenly everything else in the room began to fade away, blackness engulfing the living room, leaving only the picture being broadcast to the thirty-two-inch Zenith in Maggie O'Connell's living room.

On the screen, Alexa saw her dad.

He was dressed in his uniform and seated in one of the chairs lined up in a row behind a podium with lots of microphones coming out of it. Alexa also recognized the two men seated on either side of her dad. His boss, the sheriff, was to his left, and the district attorney was to his right. Alexa had no idea what a district attorney was, or how the man knew her father, but apparently their jobs overlapped from time to time. The man had been to their home for dinner on several occasions, and he'd even brought Alexa her own personal chocolate cake the last time after he'd learned it was her favorite. Both the sheriff and the district attorney were older than her dad, but today, as the three of them sat side by side on the platform, age seemed to melt away. Alexa couldn't quite figure out why, but to her they suddenly all looked the same. Then it hit her. She thought they all sort of looked like they were about to be sick. Like whatever reason they'd all been gathered there together was not something they wanted to participate in. They looked like they felt the way Alexa felt when she had to go to school and knew she had a big math test and had forgotten to study the night before.

The tops of heads of the crowd gathered in front of the small raised platform were just visible as the camera operator tried to zoom in a bit tighter on the man standing behind the podium, raising his hand in an effort to quiet everyone. Alexa didn't know this man, but he was wearing a suit that looked nice and his hair was combed neat and he *definitely* was older than her dad—and the sheriff and the district attorney.

The man started to speak, and while Trish O'Connell was hanging on his every word, and Maggie began tossing popcorn in the air and trying to catch it in her moth, clearly bored with the sight of a grown-up in a suit on television, Alexa Shifflett simply watched her father. She wondered if he knew she was watching right now. He wondered if he'd be upset when she told him. *If I tell him*, Alexa thought.

Her dad did not like to talk about his job with her, opting to provide only one ambiguous phrase whenever the question was asked about what he actually did all day.

"So it is with great honor," the older man in the suit said, his words slicing through Alexa's thoughts, "as mayor of this fine town, representing all of you wonderful people, that I extend my hand and offer up, with extreme gratitude and respect, my sincerest thanks to this man seated behind me. Please join me, folks, in a tremendous round of applause for the leader of this courageous task force, our very own, Officer Robert Shifflett. The man who makes sure our children are safe!"

The crowd rose to its feet and started to clap, along with the sheriff and the district attorney. Alexa watched as her dad sheepishly stood from his chair, a shy smile across his face as he stepped forward and shook the mayor's hand. Then the mayor ushered him to the podium, to the sea of awaiting microphones, and her dad said something that must have been funny, because

Alexa heard a small murmur of a chuckle trickle through the crowd.

Trish O'Connell turned and looked at Alexa, a beaming smile on her face. "You must be so proud of your father, dear." Then she turned and continued listening to Alexa's father's speech.

"What did your dad do?" Maggie asked, stuffing another fistful of popcorn into her moth.

Alexa looked at her friend and shrugged. "I have no idea."

But all she could think of was what her dad always told her when she asked what he did all day.

I catch the monsters, baby girl.

Robert Shifflett pulled his car into his driveway and waited for the garage door to open before he drove in and sat in the driver's seat and watched in the rearview as it closed shut behind him. It was a habit of his, from long before he'd even joined the police force. Something he'd seen in a movie once when he was a kid. A woman arriving home and pulling into her garage and not paying attention to the killer who'd been waiting patiently in the bushes along the side of the house and had jumped in before the door could close fully and done exactly what he'd set out to do, which was end the woman's life in a spray of blood and a dramatic swell of music.

Given Robert's profession now as an adult, the paranoia was even higher. You could never be too careful in this world. You never knew what was lurking in the bushes or waiting around the corner. You never knew what places you thought were safe might not be. You never knew who people truly were on the inside.

Robert checked the rearview again and then both the side

mirrors, scanning all around the car for any unwanted guests, and then pushed open the door to his Ford Explorer and stepped out, reaching back in across the center console to grab the pizza box from the passenger seat.

Cheese.

Alexa's favorite.

The thought of his daughter sent both a spike of love and a flood of fear through him. The spike because coming home to her was the best part of his day, each and every day. The fear because, until he could see her face with his own eyes and feel her body against his as he hugged her, he had to entertain the possibility that something might have happened to his little girl —though, she wasn't that little anymore. Hadn't been for quite some time.

He used his free hand to close the car door and then unlock the deadbolt he'd installed on the door that led into the small mudroom. Inside, he closed the door, relocked the deadbolt, and quickly punched in the code for the alarm, silencing the chime that had started to ring out through the house. He set the pizza down carefully on a wooden bench by the coatrack and then sat next to it and untied his boots, taking them off one by one and lining them up neatly with the other shoes along the wall. He saw Alexa's sneakers, a pair of Nikes he'd bought her at the start of this school year that were honestly entirely too expensive, but she'd begged and begged and the smile on her face when he'd agreed had been worth every penny. Robert was smiling now. Because the Nikes, still nearly as clean as the day he'd bought them—because that had been part of the agreement, that Alexa take care of the shoes if he were to buy them for her—sitting in the neat line with the other shoes meant that Alexa was home.

A twinge of pain shot across the left side of his head, starting right behind his eyeball and zapping its way to the back. Robert sighed and dug in his pocket for the pill bottle, found the migraine medicine and shook a tablet into his mouth. It was the most potent stuff his doctor could prescribe him, though Robert had pleaded for anything stronger—legal or not—if it would keep the migraines at bay, even just a little bit more.

They'd plagued him since he was a teenager. Blinding, white-hot, kill-me-now headaches that could cripple him for hours if not days at a time. He never left home without his bottle of pills. Never let it get close to being empty.

"Dad?"

Alexa. His angel. Calling to him from the kitchen, where he knew she'd have the plates and glasses set out on the table like she did every night he was able to come home for dinner. Robert dry-swallowed the pill, stuffed the bottle back in his pocket, and then carried the pizza into the kitchen and set it on the counter.

Alexa was sitting on one of the counter stools and flipping through a *Tiger Beat* magazine. Internally, Robert groaned. He disapproved of those types of magazines, especially for kids as young as Alexa. It was all about vanity and fame and nothing a wholesome young girl like his daughter should be worried about. He'd always refused to buy them for Alexa, but he'd not specifically forbidden them. The one she had now, she must have gotten from a friend. He considered starting a conversation with his daughter, asking her what exactly it was she found so appealing about what was essentially a gossip magazine for teens, but after the day he'd had—the hours spent with his boss and the DA prepping for the press conference and—another zap of pain in his brain—the presser itself, he was mentally exhausted and wanted nothing more than to enjoy his pizza with his daughter and then take a shower.

"Hi, baby girl," he said, sliding around the counter and wrapping his arms around her and kissing the top her head. "Good day at school?"

Alexa closed the magazine and looked him in the eye. "Yes,

121

sir. Mrs. Mallory was out sick, so we had a sub, and me and Maggie just played hangman with Michael and Jeremy."

Michael and Jeremy ... boys. Robert wasn't ready for that yet.

Robert smiled and nodded and moved the pizza box to the kitchen table, motioning for Alexa to sit and join him. "And you finished your homework at Maggie's."

"Yes, sir."

"And you came straight inside the house when they dropped you off?"

"Yes, sir."

"Good girl."

He opened the box and put a slice on Alexa's plate before dropping two onto his own. Alexa had already filled their glasses. His with water, hers with milk. To say that she and he had a comfortable routine would not be incorrect. He was very thankful to have gotten so lucky with her. Such a respectful, well-behaved, beautiful girl.

It was a shame her mother wasn't around to see it all. But, if Robert was being completely honest with himself, there was a big part of him that was *glad* Alexa's mother had run off with what's-his-name. Because it meant Robert got his little girl all to himself. Every first of Alexa's life, every milestone, every achievement, and every learning experience, it'd been him who'd been there, holding her hand every step of the way.

"Dad?"

"Yes, baby girl? How's your pizza, is it good?"

Alexa swallowed the bite she'd been chewing and nodded. "I saw you on TV today ... at Maggie's."

Goddammit. That ignorant Trish O'Connell...

"Did you now? Boy, I bet that was boring, huh? Geez, I was so embarrassed up there." He gave a big toothy grin and Alexa giggled and nodded.

"Yeah ... I mean ... yes, sir. Kinda. Maggie and I didn't really listen to much of it. But I heard that man in the suit thank you for keeping the kids safe."

Here we go ... she's going to ask.

"Yes," Robert said. "He did. It was very nice of him and all those people to come out and say thanks."

Alexa nodded and took another bite of pizza, and Robert hoped that would be the end of it, was thinking of something —*anything*—to start talking about to change the subject.

But before he could, Alexa asked, "Did you ... did you catch a monster?"

And there it is.

Robert reached for his water and took a sip. His head was starting to pound worse and he badly wanted to take another pill, but he didn't want to do it in front of Alexa, didn't want her to know he was hurting.

As a rule, he didn't talk about his job much with his daughter. She didn't need to know about all the awful things out there, waiting for her. Waiting for anyone, himself not excluded. But, because irresponsible Trish O'Connell had allowed his twelve-year-old daughter to watch a police press conference—which, if Alexa was telling the truth, she and Maggie thankfully hadn't paid much attention to—Robert could not simply pretend it had not happened.

"I did, baby girl. I did my job and those nice people thanked me. And that's enough about that."

Then he stood and placed his plate in the sink, kissed Alexa one more time atop her head and said, "I'm going to go take a shower. Daddy stinks."

[15]

LANCE WATCHED AS, AFTER THE GIRL HAD DELIVERED HER bomb (*My dad is dead.*), Murry's smile faded and his body grew rigid and he asked, "Did you say *dead?*"

The girl nodded. "Yes, sir."

And then Murry was moving. He rushed around the side of the check-in counter and headed for the door. The girl jumped back, out of the way, nearly falling into the watercooler, and Lance saw the flash of fear in her eyes.

She thought he was coming after her.

"What room?" Murry called out over his shoulder as he pulled open the door.

The girl, having regained her footing, started after Murry and said, "Five."

And then Murry was gone, the bell above the door jingling as the door slammed shut. The girl followed. Another jingling of the bell. And then it was just Lance, alone in the office. He bolted from his position behind the counter and ran for the door, jumping through it without a thought, his whole body buzzing with electricity and dizziness and—

And his feet hit the ground, and just like that he was standing on the sidewalk outside of room five, the morning air smelling sweet like honey. A Ford Explorer was parked in front of the room, dirty from travel. Murry was there, a foot or two away. He grabbed the doorknob and turned it. Found it locked and cursed, reaching into one of his pockets, then the other, coming up empty. Another curse. Followed by him pounding on the door three times with enough force to sound like thunder in the quiet morning. He yelled, "Sir, can you hear me?"

He's got a master key, Lance thought. *He left it in the office.* In reality—or rather, the present—Lance would have sprinted back to the office in search of Murry's key, doing whatever he could to help. But here, he was essentially useless.

"Here." It was the girl, suddenly right beside Lance and holding out her room key attached to the plastic key chain, just like the one Lance had been given. Lance gave her credit for remembering to grab it before she'd left the room. Couldn't imagine what it must have been like for her, waking up and finding her father dead. To keep her composure the way she was spoke volumes to her maturity.

Murry snatched the key from the girl's hand and nearly knocked the door off its hinges as he flung it open and called out, "Sir! Sir, I'm one of the owners! Can you hear me?"

Lance stepped across the threshold, grateful he wouldn't have to subject himself to another episode of "passing through." Murry was beside the bed closest to the door, saying, "Ah, shit. Ah, shit."

Lance moved to the foot of the bed and looked down at the man, who was definitely dead.

The first thing that crossed Lance's mind was the man had had a nightmare and died from fright. His arms and legs were splayed out at awkward angles—not broken, but as if he were trying to form a human swastika—like he'd been struggling against something, fighting something no longer there. His eyes were frozen wide open, blood-red from broken vessels, glossed over, lifeless. But it was his mouth that gave the true account of the man's death. His lips were slightly parted and crusty with dried vomit that looked like apple cinnamon oatmeal. The vomit had also dried in a drizzle down the side of his cheek before forming a small pool just below his chin.

Murry reached down and gently touched his fingers to the side of the man's neck—the side without the vomit, Lance noted —checking for a pulse. After a long time, long enough that Lance knew Murry was desperately pleading for the man's heart to give off a beat and turn this nightmare into something more tolerable, something that could be salvaged, he pulled his fingers away and shook his head. "Ah, shit."

Lance figured one of two things had happened. One, the man had gotten sick—drunk maybe, or taken too much of some sort of drug—and hadn't had the presence of mind to roll over once it'd started and had ended up choking to death on his own puke. Or two, he'd been poisoned and had been dying anyway while his body had fought to expel whatever toxic substance had infected it. Both options were terrible, horrific ways to die, but Lance Brody had seen enough of the evil in the world to know that either was extremely plausible. There had to be a story here, because Lance doubted very much the Universe would make the effort to drag him back in time just to show him a man die of natural causes.

Plus, there was the motel to consider. This was the fourth person Lance had seen dead since checking in. This man was part of the story.

Or maybe it's not the man ... maybe it's the—

"He's dead, right?" The girl had been standing in the

opened doorway, and Lance turned and saw her, silhouetted by the sun, take form as she walked slowly closer, one cautious step at a time, as if at any moment, the man on the bed might suddenly spring to life and shout *Gotcha!*

She had her hands pulled inside the sleeves of her sweatshirt, and it hit Lance that it was awfully warm outside for her to be wearing such heavy clothing. Pajama pants to bed were one thing, but a sweatshirt in what felt like summer?

Is she hiding something?

Lance looked back to the corpse on the bed. Considered how the girl didn't seem to be upset at all that her father was dead. Then she was there, standing right next to Lance and asking again, "Sir, he's dead, right? I ... I felt for a heartbeat, too, just like you. I didn't feel one."

What did he do to you? Lance wanted to ask. *What did your own father do?*

Murry stepped away from the head of the bed and positioned himself in such a way that he was blocking the girl's view of her father's body. "I think so, darling. I'm so sorry." Then he put a hand on her shoulder and asked, "Do you have any idea what happened?"

The girl looked briefly at Murry's hand on her shoulder, then shook her head. "No, sir. I went to sleep last night, and he was like that when I woke up."

Murry nodded. "Of course, of course. I'm so, so sorry. Come now, let's get you out of this room and we'll get this figured out, okay? Are you hungry? I'll see if my wife can make you some breakfast while I make some phone calls. Say, how old are you, anyway?"

"Twelve, sir."

Murry looked as surprised as Lance felt. "Twelve? My goodness. Aren't you a pretty thing? Come on now, I think there's some bacon and eggs left."

Murry motioned for the girl to follow him to the door, but as he took his first step, a tall figure stepped into the doorway, blotting out the light. "Wait," the figure said.

And Lance knew the voice very well.

It was the copy-and-paste boy.

[16]

(1993)

Robert Shifflett stood in the shower for a very long time. He'd washed himself thoroughly and then let the water, which he'd cranked up to just shy of scalding, beat at his muscles—his shoulders and back and neck—before he'd placed his palms flat against the front wall of the shower stall and leaned forward and let it hit him like a laser beam atop his skull. The hot water seemed to help his migraines. If he stood like this, with his head being assaulted by the near-scalding water, all the pain in his brain seemed to melt away, replaced by the oddest sense of relief that crawled out from the heat.

He thought about the day. About the press conference and all the people who'd rushed to him after it was over to shake his hand and give their thanks. "It's a team effort," he kept telling them all. "We all worked hard on this."

The reporters had been next, waiting around like vultures circling roadkill until all the regular citizens had finished picking at him and then they could swoop in for the leftovers.

The questions hit him like rapid-fire darts, the things they hadn't been able to ask during the presser, too fast and furious for him to give anybody a good answer.

Where do you go looking for these people? How do you know where to start? This is the third one you've arrested in two years. Do you think there's many more around here?

This last one almost made him chuckle, but he had the smarts not to let it through. *Many more? Of course there's many more. There's probably one among you right now.* These ignorant people thought that the criminals he and his task force went after were like finding a unicorn in the woods—something mythical and rare and hardly seen.

In reality, these monsters were more like deer. Everywhere, hiding in plain sight and waiting to jump out at you when you'd least expect it. Most of them too dumb to understand the consequences.

But Robert had done his job, doing his best to professionally answer what he could and then give the sheriff a look of gratitude when he'd finally stepped in and said he thought that was enough for now, and that they'd given out all the information they were willing to at this time.

Robert had finished up his day's work, stopped by the pizza place to grab dinner, and then driven home to his baby girl. Which was all he'd wanted to do all day. Be with her, keep her safe.

The water started to get lukewarm, and Robert was forced to abandon the relief the shower had temporarily provided. He dried off quickly, and by the time he'd put on his sweatpants and t-shirt, his head was starting to throb again, a dull ache that he knew would soon blossom into fireworks behind his eyes.

He found Alexa on the couch watching television—some weird cartoon with a talking wallaby and yellow cow that was standing upright on two legs. She'd changed into her pajamas, which at this age were baggy checked pajama pants and a tank top. Her feet were bare. Her toes painted purple. Robert stood in the doorway watching her silently for just a couple seconds, as long as he could get away with before she'd notice him standing there. He could already imagine her turning to see him, rolling her eyes and saying, "*Dad, why are you creepin'?*"

But Robert couldn't help it. He was constantly in awe of his daughter's beauty. Astonished at how big she'd gotten and—his eyes fell to the neckline of her tank top—how much she'd developed.

He put on a goofy dad grin and walked in. "Mind if I watch with you?"

She smiled back at him, and his heart nearly melted. He sat next to her and wrapped his arm around her, and she snuggled into his chest. And together they watched the silly cartoon, and Robert was never happier than he was in these moments.

Two hours later, after three cartoons and a brief reprieve of *SportsCenter* that Alexa had allowed him as her eyes had started to get heavy and Robert felt her breathing begin to change as she drifted off to sleep against his chest, Robert said it was time for bed. He watched as she stumbled half-asleep down the hall and brushed her teeth with all the enthusiasm of a zombie and then told him goodnight and that she loved him and slid into her bedroom and closed the door.

Robert felt a twinge of sadness at the sight of the closed door. It seemed like just yesterday she'd had to sleep with it open and the hallway light on because she was afraid of the dark. Robert had done what every parent does in trying to assure her there was nothing in the house that was going to get her, and that all the scary stuff she might have seen on TV was just make-believe and that she was safe.

He didn't tell her—not at that age, anyway—that the *real* monsters were other people. And they were out there, waiting for pretty girls like her.

Robert put a hand on his daughter's closed door, whispered again, *"Goodnight, baby girl,"* and then started toward the bedroom at the back of the house that he'd converted into his office. It was the farthest room from Alexa's.

His headache had subsided a bit while they'd been watching television, and he had to wonder if his love for his daughter produced some sort of chemical reaction in his body that combated the migraine. It wouldn't surprise him. Alexa was that special. But now, Robert could feel it rearing its ugly head again, its claws out and teeth sharpened, ready to bite and scratch and torment him all night long. He pulled the pill bottle from the pocket of his sweatpants and dry-swallowed two more pills. His doctor had warned him early on about taking it easy with them, how if one or two didn't work, there was no sense in taking more, it would only do more damage than good.

Robert didn't care. Maybe it was a placebo effect, but in his head, more pills meant more chances of relief.

He opened the door to his office and switched on the lights. Shut the door behind him and locked it, checked to make sure the blackout curtains were still in place on the window, double-checked the door lock again, and then crossed the room and sat at the computer desk.

The sheriff's department had developed the task force a little over two years ago, and when Robert had been asked if he'd liked to be assigned to it—one of the very few the sheriff felt completely confident in asking, he'd been told—Robert's heart rate had kicked up and a surge of adrenaline had rushed through his veins and he'd agreed before he had fully realized the possibilities.

Or the consequences.

He was propelled by his eagerness to prove himself, maybe get a promotion, a pay raise.

And also by his need to avoid getting caught. By the department *and* the bad guys. By saying yes, he'd instantly become somewhat of a double agent. Both the fish, and the fisherman.

And it had been easier than he'd ever imagined. Robert was smart, careful and calculated. He lived in the world of shadows, where the very monsters he was hunting showed off their prey, blended in and acted as if he belonged. Shared their trophies, and he shared with them his own.

But he was different. He knew that. Deep down, his motivations were much more poetic than the carnal desires and fantasies of his fellow shadow-dwellers. The language they used when discussing their shared interests was so crude and vulgar and simply unsophisticated.

Robert was in it for the beauty. Marveled over how purity and innocence could mesh together to form such magnificent, gorgeous bodies. To Robert, the whole thing was about the art. About capturing life's greatest specimens and putting them on display.

And it was this viewpoint that allowed him to rise himself above his fellow men and women—because yes, there were women among the shadows, too—and use his intelligence and his resources to seamlessly coexist in both their world and his own, to fulfill his own desires of love and purity and respect while also exposing the most vile and disgusting creatures among the crowd and subtly luring them into the arms of the law, where society would judge them accordingly and they would pay oh so dearly for their misguided philosophies.

Computers and the Internet had been the game-changer.

Without them, Robert's success and ability to live in both worlds would have been drastically diminished. In the old way, telegrams and coded letters and phone calls from pay phones and secret drop spots behind dumpsters and rendezvous exchanges in secluded public locations had been the way of life. You had to be *present*, you had to go *out* to get the goods. To meet people. To conduct business.

But now, you could do it all from behind a locked door in a room at the back of your house, behind an alias, aka username, that didn't betray a single identifying detail about yourself if you didn't want it to. Instead of the letters and telegrams and phone calls, now there were chat rooms and message boards and the Mosaic web browser. Instead of manila folders sealed away in garbage bags and zippered freezer bags duct-taped to known drop spots, now there were privately hosted FTP severs that could hold the contents of a thousand manila folders, sitting patiently and secure, waiting for anyone who had the key to come inside and look around.

And you never had to go rooting around in some trash can in a public park to get to it. You just had to punch a few keys on the keyboard and you had it all.

Robert fired up the computer and waited for his modem to connect and then quickly checked a few or his favorite message boards, just scanning to see if there was anything—or *anybody*—new or of interest. Of course, he wasn't supposed to be conducting any sort of official police business off-duty, especially work related to the task force, for obvious reasons. But, hey, it was because of *him* that the task force had had any success at all.

Robert felt no guilt. He was one of the good guys.

Exhausted and ready for sleep, he was about to shut the computer down and head to bed when a ferocious stab of pain shot through his head, making him double over and cry out

136

softly. He reached for the pill bottle in his pocket and then looked back to the computer screen.

Besides the hot showers and the pills, there was another thing that always caused temporary relief, allowed his mind to drift away from the pain.

Robert used the mouse and clicked through some of his onscreen folders until he located his special one. His most favorite. The most beautiful of his collection. He opened a few of the files and instantly felt himself begin to grow hard. Slipped a hand beneath the waist of his sweatpants.

When he was finished, he cleaned up, shut down the computer, and then went to bed.

He said a prayer, thanking the Lord for another day of keeping his daughter safe.

[17]

THE COPY-AND-PASTE BOY, HIS LOOMING FIGURE IN THE
doorway stepping forward and coming fully into view, didn't
even glance at the dead body on the motel room's bed. He didn't
look at Murry, and of course he didn't look at Lance. Though
Lance wished he would have. Wished the boy would notice him
and introduce himself and say, "Hey there, we sure do have a lot
to talk about."

Instead, the boy's focus was completely dedicated to the girl,
who'd turned around at the sound of the boy's voice.

"*Wait*," he'd said.

And they had. All three of them.

He stepped into the room and gave the girl the gentlest of
smiles. Her face lit up in return, the first real bit of emotion
Lance had seen from her. As if the tall and lanky stranger with
the sharp cheekbones coming to join them was the Prince
Charming she'd been waiting for. And in some way that Lance
knew he would not be able to explain or articulate, he figured
maybe the boy was. He might not have ridden to her on a
gallant steed, climbed a tower or slain a dragon, but at some
level he might be there to rescue her, all the same. From what

Lance had already seen of the boy's past, and based on the conversation he'd overheard between the boy and Meriam, Lance doubted very much that the boy was here in this room by accident.

Then, with a creeping feeling of stark understanding, a trickle of dread that wove into his thoughts, Lance turned and looked back to the body on the bed. The girl's dead father.

Maybe there was *a dragon slain*, Lance thought. *But how, and by whom? The boy?*

"Hi," the boy said, collapsing down onto one knee so he could be more at eye level with the girl. "What's your name?"

The girl's entire physique seemed to soften, her muscles relaxing. Maybe it was because the boy was closer to her own age than Murry, some level of comfort that would only be achieved via a peer. Or maybe it was just because the boy was the boy, whatever that meant. But Lance knew it meant *something.*

"I'm Alexa," the girl said.

The boy nodded as if this made perfect sense, of course she was an Alexa, she *looked* like an Alexa. But Lance thought the nod meant something else. Lance thought the nod was because the boy clearly already knew exactly who this girl was.

"Alexa. Hey, that's a really cool name!" the boy said. "Do people ever call you Lexie?"

The girl crinkled her face, like she'd tasted something rotten. "No way."

The boy smiled. "Oh, thank goodness. Alexa is way better."

The girl laughed. "I agree."

Then the boy stuck out his hand and said, "Alexa, my name's Quinten, but everybody calls me Quint."

Finally, a name! With all the mystery surrounding the boy, Lance could at least start thinking of him with an actual name. One less thing to try and figure out.

"Like that fisherman guy from *Jaws*?" the girl asked, cocking her head to one side.

The boy—Quinten—looked over to Murry with wide eyes and actually laughed out loud, a short bark of a laugh that echoed through the room. "That's exactly who I was named after. My mom loved that movie," Quinten said. Then added, "Smart girl."

Alexa giggled and shook Quinten's hand.

And Lance saw it. Saw the handshake last a bit longer than normal, saw the quick blankness flash across Quinten's face. Saw the boy's features fall back into their pleasant normalcy as he broke contact with the girl and moved to stand.

And Lance thought that, despite his good-natured attempt, Quinten looked a little more somber than he had when he first entered the room.

"Hey," he said. "Alexa, tell you what. It's getting a little weird in here, and I know my uncle has some things he needs to do to take care of everything, so I have an idea. I'm about to go get some breakfast at this diner in town with my good friend Julie. She's hilarious and I think you'd love her. You want to come hang out with us for a while? Best pancakes and waffles you'll ever eat."

Lance thought about raising his hand and asking if he could come, too. He enjoyed waffles and pancakes as much as the next guy. And he could use some coffee.

Alexa turned her head and looked at Murry, her eyes asking.

Murry, seeming to realize she was asking his permission, shot a look to Quinten and must have seen all he needed to because he quickly said, "Hey, that sounds like a great idea. I'm a bit jealous myself. I could go for some pancakes."

Amen, Lance thought.

Alexa looked back to Quinten, smiling. "Good, I'm *starved*."

"Great! Tell you what, is that your suitcase over there?" He

141

pointed to a small rolling suitcase on the floor by the television stand, its lid zipped shut.

Alexa nodded.

"Okay, thought so. Do you have anything in the bathroom? Toothbrush, shampoo, anything like that?"

Alexa nodded, beginning to turn back around in a direction that would put her in line of sight to her dead father on the bed. Quinten reached out before she could and gently grabbed her shoulders and stopped her. Unlike when Murry had placed the hand on her shoulder earlier, Alexa did not seem to react to Quinten's touch so much as obey it. "Tell you what, why don't you go down to the office—my aunt Meriam should be down there—and wait while I gather up your things and bring them to you so can you get dressed and we can go? Sound good?"

And there was a look of relief on the girl's face, like maybe she understood this was it, she'd never have to see the inside of this motel room again. "Sounds good," she said.

And then Quinten stood and took her hand and led her out to the sidewalk. Lance was about to follow, but only a few seconds passed before Quinten was back in the room, closing the door behind him and walking right up to the edge of the bed and looking down at the dead man.

And nobody spoke. Outside on the road, a large delivery truck roared by. Nobody even glanced at it. Murry stood back with his hands clasped behind his back, watching his nephew. Waiting. Understanding on some level that this might be about more than just a man getting sick and dying.

Lance understood this, too, and was as eager to hear what the boy would say next as Murry was. More so, in fact.

After a minute, maybe two, Quinten's eyes seemed to come back into focus. He looked to Murry and said, "We need to get rid of him?"

"What?" Murry said, not surprised, but as if he hadn't heard correctly.

"Don't call the police. Don't report this. We've got to get rid of him and never speak about it again."

"When you say 'get rid of him,' you mean—"

"Dispose of the body, yes."

Murry waited a beat. Said, "You're sure about this?" Which Lance thought was an incredibly calm response for a regular person who'd just been asked to improperly dispose of a corpse without notifying the authorities. But, Lance had to assume that Murry, just like Meriam, understood that his nephew possessed otherworldly gifts. Would do things and, in the case of today, ask things of others that they would not fully understand.

"You need to trust me," Quinten said.

Murry sighed, as if the boy had played a trump card and he knew he'd lost the battle. And then, with very little conviction, offered, "We can't just..."

"We'll figure it out."

"What about the girl?" Murry asked.

"You need to trust me. You'll see." Then Quinten rounded the front of the bed, Lance having to step back several steps in order to keep the boy from passing through him, and he made his way to room's second bed, where he pulled the comforter off and then draped it over the dead man's body, keeping those bloodshot eyes from staring into nothing any longer.

"What happened to him?" Murry asked. "Do you know?"

Lance, along with Murry, was waiting for an answer. He had been staring at the vague outline of the dead man's body beneath the comforter when Murry had asked the question, trying to put the pieces together himself as to what exactly had happened to cause the man to die, and what exactly had happened between the man and his daughter, when the silence that had followed had suddenly grown much too long.

Lance looked up and found Quinten standing just a few feet away, staring directly at him.

And Lance was hit with a rush of both fear and excitement. Fear because he didn't know what it meant for Quinten to be able to see him—was he supposed to be seen? Would this somehow change the past, alter history? Was this all part of the Universe's plan?

Excitement because if the boy could see Lance, there was a chance he might be able to hear Lance, too. And if he could hear Lance, then maybe he could answer some questions. Lance didn't even know how to begin such a conversation. *Hi, you don't know me, but I'm ... well, I think you and I are very much alike. I have special abilities, too. Oh, and I'm from the future.*

Quinten's eyes were focused on where Lance was standing, but there was a lack of focal point all the same. Maybe he wasn't seeing him at all. To test this, Lance started waving both his hands in the wildly in the air, like a half-drunk fan at a basketball game trying to catch a t-shirt being shot out of an air cannon.

Quinten moved closer, slowly, as if his mere disturbance of the air might ruin whatever it was he was working toward. Lance stopped moving. Waited to see what would happen.

"Quint?" It was Murry, sounding concerned. "Everything okay?"

Quinten ignored him and then did something that sent Lance into panic mode. He raised his right hand and started to reach out, fingers mere inches from Lance's own chest. He moved to take the last step, the step that would force his presence into the space that Lance occupied in some time and dimension that wasn't truly this one.

And Lance quickly stepped to the side and the boy's hand reached out and hit nothing but the television.

Lance couldn't help it. Passing through doors was one thing.

He wasn't ready to have a human being pass through him. The thought of it creeped him out.

When his fingers hit the darkened television screen, Quinten seemed to snap out of whatever trance he'd fallen into, quickly turning back around the finding his uncle staring.

"Sorry, what?" the boy asked.

"Everything okay?"

"Oh, yeah. I just ... I thought I. Never mind. It's hard to explain."

Murry sighed. "Usually is, huh?"

"You asked me something, didn't you?"

Murry nodded. "Yes. I asked if you know what happened to him?" He pointed to the body shape under the comforter.

"Not entirely. At least, not in a way I can understand yet. But I'll just tell you this: he got what he deserved."

Murry didn't seem to like this answer very much. "Is any man really to judge another man to be deserving of death?"

Quinten shook his head. "Maybe not, Uncle. But there are greater things than man that do the judging." He reached down and grabbed Alexa's suitcase, started for the door and then stopped. "Oh, and Murry, this guy was a cop. I imagine people will start looking for him sooner rather than later, so we need to come up with something good."

And then the boy slipped out the door and left Murry and Lance with the dead man on the bed and a room full of unanswered questions.

[18]

(1993)

He did not keep the room locked, but he did have a password on the computer.

Alexa sat in her father's office chair in the back bedroom, facing the computer screen and watching the cursor blink blink blink at her, waiting for an attempt.

He'd never specifically forbidden her to come in here on her own, but Alexa could feel the guilt—no, that wasn't quite right; it was *anxiety*—begin swelling in her chest as she'd made her way down the hallway and grabbed the doorknob and turned it and pushed through the door and made her way to the computer desk. Each step had increased the beating of her heart.

Because, even at twelve years old, Alexa knew she was on the verge of something. She was about to go poking around in the life of not just an adult, but her own *father*, and something tugging at her gut, like a string being pulled just behind her belly button, made her think that whatever she might discover

147

in this room would be an enlightening moment of a grand scale. Like finally being able to pull back the curtain on some tremendous secret and peer into the truth for the first time.

She was excited. Yes, there was definitely a sense of giddiness mixed in with the anxiety.

Excited for the secret. Anxious that she might get caught. And what would that mean, if he caught her? What would that do to their relationship? Would he be mad? Would he ever trust her again?

It was a gamble, going into the office and powering up the computer. But Alexa had to roll the dice. Something had changed in her. For so long she'd been able to go along with her father's vagueness about his job as a policeman and accepted his answer—which, now at twelve years old, she'd started to recognize as avoidance—about hunting monsters. She figured that like most adults, her father thought that this type of dismissive answer was *for her own good*. Adults always acted like that. Like Alexa and her friends were still just little kids running around in their diapers and had to be shielded from anything other than cartoons on the television and could be placated with nothing more than a cookie and a juice box. The adults had their own world, and the sign on the door read No Kids Allowed.

Which, for the most part, was fine with Alexa and her friends. They lived in their own world, too. Alexa had secrets of her own. Like the fact that she had kissed two different boys this year at school—one at an afterschool dance with the lights turned down low and the teachers' backs turned just long enough for his lips to find hers, and the other at Allison Varney's thirteenth birthday party, where they'd all been gathered in Allison's basement with cups of soda and music playing and hormones ripping across the room like an F5 tornado.

And also the fact that she'd gotten her period. Though this secret she'd only kept from her dad, mostly out of embarrassment. It was one of only a handful of times in her life she'd wished that her mother had not left them, that there was another female in their house. She'd gone to Maggie's mom instead, and Trish had helped her, gotten her what she needed and explained what to do—all with Maggie giggling and snickering at Alexa's side. Alexa had made Trish swear she wouldn't tell her dad. Trish protested at first but eventually agreed. And Alexa knew she'd kept her word, because something like that ... her dad would have *definitely* talked to her about.

And that was the thing. Her father loved to talk about *her*, loved to attempt to have Alexa tell him everything about her life, paint him a complete picture of her every waking day. He'd backed off a bit as she'd gotten older, realizing that along with her age there had to come some sense of privacy, but she could tell it bothered him. But...

But he never talked about himself.

He was her provider and her protector. He was her father.

But Alexa had suddenly come to realize she had no idea who he was.

It was the press conference that had finally pulled at the thread of this realization until it completely unraveled and exposed itself. A crowd full of people that seemed to know much more about her own dad than Alexa did. And when she'd try to ask him about it ... same old answers, same old change the subject.

He'd made her do what she was about to do. She deserved more.

So after school, she'd ridden the bus home instead of heading to Maggie's, and after searching every other room of the house—she knew it was silly, but the anxiety had already been creeping in— to make sure her father wasn't hiding from her, she walked straight back to the office and booted up the computer.

She was good with computers. They had computer lab once a week at school, and she could type faster than most of her classmates. And instead of playing the games like the rest of her friends, she liked to go clicking around on the screen, exploring all the different applications and features.

And she was ready to go exploring now.

Except she hadn't thought about there being a password.

In hindsight, she should have. If her father worked so hard to keep things from her in the rest of his life, why wouldn't he have protected any information that was just lying around the house?

Alexa had been staring at the cursor for what felt like an eternity. Blink, blink, blink. She'd tried typing in PASSWORD and of course that had been wrong. Blink, blink, blink. She'd tried the numbers for her dad's birthday and that had been wrong, too. Blink, blink, blink. And then she'd tried her own birthday, which had also been wrong, but had also given her a spark of inspiration. To listen to her dad talk, whether to her or to other adults, Alexa was his pride and joy, the apple of his eye, his reason for living, all the sappy things any parent will say about their own children.

She was the person always on his mind.

She typed ALEXA and hit the Enter key.

It was wrong.

Blink, blink, blink.

Alexa felt her excitement begin to wane and she suddenly wanted to cry. Cry because she had failed. Cry because all she wanted was for her own father to be honest with her, and instead she had to go snooping around like a thief.

A single tear escaped and began to slide down her cheek.

Don't cry, baby girl. She heard her dad's words in her head, the same thing he always said when he saw her with tears in her eyes. *It'll all be okay. Don't cry, baby g—*

Alexa sat up hard in the chair, using the back of her hand to quickly wipe away the fallen tear. She typed BABYGIRL and hit Enter.

She was in.

All the anxiety was erased, the excitement winning the battle and taking over. She was in. She'd cracked the code and she was in. She was proud of herself, floating on a cloud of achievement. Her hand found the mouse and she began the hunt, clicking into folders, her eyes scanning the file names and looking for anything that would give her answers. She didn't know for certain that her dad did any police work at home on this computer, but if he did, she was going to find it. If he didn't, she'd find whatever else he had stored on the hard drive, any shred of evidence of the man he was.

What she found stunned her into absolute stillness, her hands freezing over keyboard and mouse. Her breath hitching in her chest. Her eyes unblinking.

She'd found a folder named FAVORITE CASES, which had instantly excited her. *Finally*, she'd thought. *I'm going to see what he does. And these are his favorites!*

Inside this folder had been several others, all with folder names consisting or random numbers. *Case numbers*, she'd thought. Though she had no idea if that was an actual thing. It had just made sense at the time.

She clicked inside one of the folders and found it full of picture files. She recognized the file type because it was the type of files they saved at school when the teacher told them to draw something in the Paint application. She clicked on the first picture file and waited for it to open.

And then it did.

And that's when she froze. Unable to breathe, unable to think.

It was a picture of a girl, maybe around Alexa's own age.

Maybe a bit younger. She was in a bedroom. The walls painted pink. She stood at chest of drawers, pulling out a shirt.

She was completely naked.

Alexa, when her body finally released itself from its prison, quickly closed the image. Her mind reeling as it processed what she'd just seen.

She clicked the back arrow at the top of the window and then stared at the list of folders again. *They can't be*, she thought. *They all can't be.*

She opened another folder, found that it too was full of image files. She forced herself to open one and then gasped when she saw it was a picture of a young boy. He couldn't be any older than ten at the most, and he was also not wearing any clothes.

She closed this file so fast the mouse nearly slid from beneath her hand. She clicked the back arrow again and was back at the list of folders.

Alexa's head was swimming, her heart racing. Her mind was a blur of questions and confusion and...

And she felt sick.

She closed her eyes and counted to ten. Took deep breaths. Waited for the wave of nausea to pass.

When it did, she opened her eyes and looked at the screen. She stared blankly at the list of folders, not really seeing them. She knew what she needed to do. She needed to shut down the computer and leave the room and never ever say a word to anybody about what she'd just seen.

But what *had* she seen? Who were those kids, and why did her dad have *those* pictures?

And why where there so many?

It didn't matter. That's what she decided. Right now the pictures didn't matter at all. All that mattered was her getting out of there right this second.

And then, as she was moving the mouse to click the button to shut the computer down, she noticed the name of one of the folders.

At first, it was just random numbers.

To anyone else, they would have remained random numbers.

But to Alexa, when she looked more closely and separated them out in her head, they became a number she was very familiar with.

Her birthday.

No, she thought. *Impossible.*

She hesitated. Tried to convince herself that it was nothing except a coincidence and whatever was inside that folder had absolutely nothing to do with her. But she failed. She knew that if she didn't look, she'd spend the rest of the day, the week, her life, wondering if she was wrong.

She moved the mouse and opened the folder and saw it was full of image files.

She clicked and opened one.

It loaded.

And Alexa stared at a picture of herself in the bathroom that was right down the hall from where she was sitting, just stepping out of the shower.

Her entire world collapsed.

"Alexa?"

She spun around in the chair and found her father standing in the doorway.

[19]

LANCE WAITED ONLY A FEW SECONDS BEFORE HE STARTED to move across room five's carpet, wanting to see if the Universe would allow him to walk through the door and follow Quinten and the young girl, Alexa. Lance knew there was going to be more to that story, more about the girl, but he wasn't sure he was supposed to know the details.

And honestly, despite his normal sense of moral obligation to follow up on such things, all Lance really wanted to do was learn more about Quinten. He wanted to talk to him for hours, preferably over many cups of coffee, and discuss the boy's entire life. Birth to the present. What were Quinten's abilities? How were he and Lance similar, and maybe more importantly, how were they different?

Lance did not feel too guilty about disregarding his further interest in the girl. After all, Quinten had seemed to have had things under control. Plus, the man on the bed was still dead, and Lance figured that whatever the girl's problem had been to begin with, it had died with him.

Lance was a step away from the motel room's door when somebody dimmed the lights inside the room.

No, that wasn't right. Lance stopped and looked to the window, to where the curtains had been pulled shut. There was no longer any trace of the morning light slipping in along the edges.

Lance turned around and found the room to be completely different.

Murry was gone. The girl, Alexa, was lying on the far bed, dressed in the same baggy sweatshirt and pajama pants she'd been wearing before. Her eyes were focused on the television set, which had been turned on and tuned to a rerun of *I Love Lucy*.

The man who had been dead when Lance had first entered the room was now alive. Sitting up in bed and reading a paperback novel in the light from the bedside lamp. There was an amber pill bottle on the nightstand next to the phone, and Lance could swear it hadn't been there in the scene before, the scene where the man had been dead. He remembered the dried vomit and wondered where the pill bottle had ended up.

What wasn't seen, but to Lance was as palpable as if somebody had been announcing it from a megaphone, was the tension lingering in the air between the girl and her father. Lance watched for several minutes, and every so often the man's eyes would glance sideways, abandoning the words on the paperback's pages and staring at his daughter for several seconds at a time. Once, he actually looked up, as if he'd suddenly gotten an idea and was about to speak, but then he quickly looked like he'd decided better of it and went back to reading.

The girl's eyes never left the television screen. In fact, she hardy moved at all.

The show went to a commercial break and the man set the paperback on the bed and swung his legs off the side. The girl instantly reacted, flinching and sitting upright and beginning to shift toward the far side of the bed.

The man stopped moving, looked at his daughter with something like disbelief, and then hung his head in sadness. "You don't have to be afraid of me," he said. "I'm your father."

The girl didn't respond, and the man stood and went to the bathroom. Once the door was closed, Alexa visibly relaxed, sinking back into the pillows of the bed and watching the television.

And then there was a flicker of the power.

At least, that was the best way Lance could process it. It was as if the power had surged and then flickered off and on, just a microsecond of the room being swallowed in darkness, barely perceptible. And then everything came back into focus and the room was much darker, the bedside lamp was turned off and there was only the glow of the television casting shadows about the walls.

Both Alexa and the man were asleep. The girl was buried deep beneath the comforter, the hood of her sweatshirt pulled up and the drawstrings tight, as if she were trying to protect every square inch of her skin. She was curled up on the far end of the bed, facing the wall.

The man was on his back, his own comforter pulled up to his chest, his mouth slightly open, a steady purr that might have eventually graduated into a snore wheezing from his throat. But it never got the chance. Because then she was there.

As if the darkness had gathered its energy and been able to form itself into a tangible shape, the dead woman from room one materialized slowly, like a Polaroid picture developing in the empty space between the two beds. She was still wearing the clothes she'd died in, the same flannel pajamas she'd worn when Lance had seen her hanging from the bedsheet. She stood in the empty space between the beds, unmoving, staring down at the man, who was fast asleep. Then the woman turned around, moved to face Alexa. She took a small step forward, reached out a hand toward the girl, fingers splayed and wanting, desperately desiring a touch. Then her body heaved in what Lance thought might have been a sob of resignation, and the woman spun back around toward the man, fury in her spirit eyes.

Lance found he was confused. He knew that he himself was alive in a different time, somehow allowed by the Universe to witness these events, unclear as to in what manner he was actually existing right here and now, but he wasn't sure in what element or time the spirit of the woman from room one was existing. Was she part of the past? Was Lance seeing her just part of his witnessing a previous time? Or was she here now, with him, able to form herself in whichever time and space she wanted, seeing things, like him, fresh and new?

Lance got his answer immediately.

The woman leaned forward and put her face close to the side of the man's head, right by his ear.

And instantly the man's hands flew from his side and grabbed his head, his left wrist and forearm passing right through the woman's shoulders and neck and face. He began to thrash, the comforter flying this way and that, legs flailing. "No, no, no, no, no," the man mumbled in gasping, broken breaths.

His head and torso shook from side to side, his hands clamped viselike to the sides of his skull. He tried to sit up twice, frantic thrusts of his upper body, but it was as if he was weighted down by something unseen, a great force knocking him back to the pillows. "No, no, no. I'm sorry, I'm sorry, I'm sorry." More words forced through lips that were pursed in a grimace of pain. "No, no, *no!*"

And with every move, every change of direction and every desperate flail of his body, the man could not escape the woman's ... what? Attack?

To Lance, it looked like she was doing nothing more than whispering in the man's ear.

And as he moved, it was as though she were attached to him, shackled together, glued to his ear. Her image moved and mimicked his every action, as though she knew every step of his dance an instant before the man did and she was right there waiting for him.

"Okay, okay, okay! No more!"

These words the man had actually summoned the strength to yell. His left hand shot out toward the nightstand and grabbed the bottle of pills, and with a practiced motion, he spun the top off and it landed on the comforter, and the man was dumping the entire bottle of pills into his pleading mouth. He looked like a baby bird reaching up for the worm being dangled by its mother.

The man chewed and crunched and gagged and swallowed each and every pill, letting the pill bottle fall from his hand and come to rest on the bed.

And then the man lay still, flat on his back, his chest heaving as he tried to catch his breath. Eventually the breathing slowed, falling back into a steady, calm rhythm. As if everything were finally over and the man was once again at peace.

But then he got sick. A choked gagging sound escaped his mouth and at once he moved to sit up. But he couldn't. The woman leaned in closer, as if she were pressing down, and the man began to cough and gag some more and then the vomit came, a small geyser that went airborne a couple inches and then landed *splat* back onto his face. More choking, though becoming more muffled. More thrashing and attempts to move, all met with unseen resistance.

And then the man was still, his chest no longer rising or falling with breath.

The woman was gone.

The room was still.

And then, as if witnessing a time-lapse video, everything

sped up to what looked like 1000x speed and the sun was back, fighting through the window curtains and then crossing the floor and climbing the wall.

It was morning again.

Time returned to normal speed and Alexa sat up and moved to sit on the edge of her own bed and looked at her dead father. She sat that way for a long time, and Lance took a few steps closer, wanting to really see her face.

And what he saw in the girl's eyes, in all her features, was relief. She didn't even look the slightest bit shocked, or worried, or upset, or surprised, or ... *anything.*

She looked calm. Knowing.

She stood from the bed and walked to her father, her eyes falling down to the comforter where the empty pill bottle and its lid were lying just inches from the man's cold hand. Then she reached out and picked them both up, securing the lid, and placed the bottle in the pocket of her pajama pants. Then she said something Lance didn't understand but recognized as a farewell. "I guess the monsters won."

Alexa walked around the bed, switching off the television as she passed it, and opened the motel room's door and made a right turn, heading for the office.

Lance knew where she was going. He'd already seen this part.

But he followed her anyway. He knew he was finished in room five.

A step away from the door, Lance froze, his senses picking up something. Another change in the room. Something shifting. He turned around and found the dead man still lying back on the bed, but his head was lifted just slightly, turned in Lance's direction. His bloodshot eyes stared through Lance and when he spoke, flecks of dried vomit fell from his cracked lips.

"He'll be waiting."

Lance nodded. "So I've been told."

He turned and walked out the door.

[20]

(1993)

Alexa was pretending to be asleep in the motel room.

She'd not slept well ever since that day, the day he'd found her snooping on his computer. At home that night, she'd gone to bed and locked the bedroom door and used all her strength to slide her dresser in front of it. She knew he'd heard it, the sound it made sliding against the wall, her grunts of effort as her arms and back had strained. But he'd said nothing. Let her be.

He knew he'd messed up. He knew he'd done something he could never take back. Something had been broken between them. No, not broken. Shattered to pieces, a million tiny slivers that no amount of restoration would ever repair. Alexa felt this, but she was not sad. A blanket woven of disgust and revulsion kept out all other emotion. Thick and heavy and wrapping her in such a tight embrace it was nearly suffocating. She'd lain on her bed that night, crying rivers into her pillow. Scared and alone.

Because who could she tell? Who could get her dad in trouble? He was a police officer, after all. She thought about all those people who'd gathered at the press conference, how they'd clapped for her dad and how the man in the suit had looked so proud as he'd thanked him and welcomed him to the podium. Her dad was a hero. And who was she? Who would believe her? The word of a silly twelve-year-old against a monster hunter.

Honestly, she wasn't even sure she could fully articulate what had been so wrong about what had happened in the office after he'd caught her. All she'd known was that it had triggered something inside her, some inherent warning system that had screamed at her, that sent waves of every bad emotion through her bloodstream, stirred the pot in her stomach, threatening it to boil over with sick.

Violation. That was the word that popped into her head. An adult word that she'd heard from time to time but had never had any context in her own life to which to apply it. She didn't know exactly what it meant, but she knew it fit.

I've been violated, she thought to herself. That was what she would tell someone.

But who? The man in the suit? He had seemed important. But how could she find him? She didn't even know his name.

She stayed in her room all the next day. She'd had to move the dresser to go to the bathroom, but she'd sprinted across the hall and locked the bathroom door behind her and then sprinted back when she was finished. She left the dresser where it was this time, settling for just locking the door. Instead, she opened her window and kicked out the screen, letting it fall into the bushes a few inches below. An escape route, if her dad came in and ... and what? Tried something?

He didn't go to work. She'd not heard the garage door open and close or the alarm set. The phone rang midmorning, and she heard him answer it in the kitchen. The school calling. Her dad saying, "Yes, she's not feeling too well this morning. Yes, I'm sure she'll be back tomorrow if she's feeling better."

And then silence for hours.

Around noon her stomach growled, and she knew she'd have to eat eventually. Would have to leave the room. She looked to her window and wondered how long it would take him to realize she was gone.

She didn't get the chance.

He knocked gently on the door. She didn't answer. Fear seized her heart.

"Alexa, please open the door."

She didn't move. Was rooted to her bed.

"Alexa. Open the door. I have something to tell you."

This time, the doorknob jiggled as he turned it, testing it.

And then there was no warning, just the door suddenly flying open, bits of the door frame splintering from the wall. The sound scared her more than anything, and she'd jumped from the bed, her only thought being to jump out the window.

But he caught her. She'd barely left the mattress before one of his hands grabbed her shoulder and stopped her. His grip was firm, too tight, but there was something gentle about the way he slowly pulled her back, turning her and sitting her on the bed to face him.

She started to cry.

He reached up and wiped a tear from her face. "Don't cry, baby girl. Everything's going to be fine. We're going to take a trip, you and I, what do you say about that? It's been a while, right? Too long since we've had a vacation. I've been working too hard and ... well, I just think we both need a little relaxation and fun, right? Would you agree?"

Alexa knew it wouldn't matter if she agreed or not.

She could still feel his grip on her shoulder from where he'd grabbed her. A phantom pain that would forever be a reminder of how things had changed. He'd never touched her with such force. Had never so much as laid a hand on her in her entire life. Not a swat on the bottom or anything more. She knew then, as he kneeled down only a foot away from her, that wherever he wanted to go, she was going to have to go with him.

But maybe that was better. Maybe out in the world, she'd find a way to get help. Maybe a plan would come to her. Maybe she'd find the right person to tell.

She had to believe these things, had to have hope. She'd made the decision right there on her bed at twelve years old that what had happened in her father's office would not be the end of her. Would not define her.

Somebody would help her, and she'd know them when she saw them.

They'd ended up here at this motel. He'd made her pack her suitcase and they'd taken off, pulling out of the garage with Alexa staring at their house with an odd sense of mourning. *Goodbye*, she'd thought.

They'd driven for the remainder of the day and then straight through the night, with Alexa dozing off and on in the passenger seat and her father stopping at gas stations for fill-ups and huge to-go cups full of coffee. Dinner had been at a McDonald's drive-thru, and at one of the fill-up stops he'd purchased an assortment of snack food and sodas and bottles of water, telling her to help herself to whatever she wanted. In the ugly yellow light shining down on them at one of the gas stations, the clock on the dash saying it was just after three in the morning, Alexa cracked open a bottle of water and took a sip, daring a glance at her dad as he munched on a bag of pretzels. For the briefest of moments, she thought he looked scared. Which provoked the thought, *Are we running? Is he trying to run away from what happened?* And that shard of hope that she'd demanded herself to cling onto grew larger. *If he's running, he thinks he might get in trouble.*

It was the first time in her life her father had appeared vulnerable to Alexa.

But then, a more foreboding thought followed. An alternative viewpoint that worked to squeeze the shard of hope back down to its original size and maybe cause it to disappear altogether. *He's taking me away so I can't tell anybody. He'll never let me tell anybody.*

They drove on. Another McDonald's drive-thru for breakfast, a Burger King for lunch, and then midafternoon, her dad had made a sudden exit from the interstate and then they'd been traveling down a rural road that became so desolate it seemed as though it were a mistake to be there in the first place.

"Getting tired," he'd mumbled from the driver's seat. A bit of ketchup had dried on the corner of his mouth. "I think we've gone far enough for now."

Alexa stared out the window at the trees and fields and the setting sun dipping along the horizon and thought, *Unless you brought a tent or want to sleep in the car, we better go a little bit farther.*

They rounded a bend in the road and there it was. A motel, spawned from nothing, waiting for them on the side of the road. Six rooms. No other cars.

"Perfect!" her dad had said, a spark of energy causing him to sit up straight and widen his eyes. "Just what we need."

And Alexa found herself agreeing with him. She didn't know why, but something about the sight of the motel made her suddenly feel ... happy? Yes, that was part of it, but not everything. There was another feeling being brought forth the closer they got to the building as her father pulled into the parking area and nosed the car up in front of the door to the motel's office. It made her feel...

"Safe," she whispered under her breath. It was the first word she'd said in their entire trip, the first word she'd said period since that day in his office, and the sound of her voice caused her father's head to swivel around hard in her direction, his eyes ablaze with excitement. Like maybe his plan was working, maybe she was coming around to forgetting the whole thing had ever happened.

"What's that, baby girl?"

Alexa said nothing. Crossed her arms and stared straight ahead.

He told her to stay in the car while he got them a room.

They were given room five, and once they'd gone inside, Alexa had changed into a sweatshirt and pajama pants, desperately wanting to shed the clothes she'd been sitting in for the last twenty-four hours. Outside, the summer air was warm, and the motel room was stuffy. Alexa didn't care about the heat. She kept the sweatshirt on and the sleeves pulled down and her hood up.

She didn't want any part of her exposed for her dad to see.

They'd settled in, he with his paperback novel and she staring blankly at the television screen, trying to let her mind focus on what she was watching, but failing. She badly wanted to float away with a mindless television show, let the laugh track and onscreen antics cause her to forget, if just for a moment, the turn her life had taken.

She couldn't do it. Not entirely. Couldn't seem to shake the fear that was clinging to her, that notion that at any moment, her father would come to her, do it again. With every move he made, Alexa found herself flinching, sliding further away from him.

Finally, he fell asleep.

Alexa switched off the bedside lamp but left the television on with the volume turned down. She didn't want to be in complete darkness. She wanted to be able to see him if he came to her, wanted the shadows to sway with his movement, an early warning signal.

She cinched the hood of her sweatshirt and buried herself beneath the covers, then turned to face the wall, putting her back to him, not even wanting him to see her face should he wake.

She told herself she wouldn't sleep. Wouldn't give him the benefit of being able to sneak up on her. But within minutes, she was dreaming.

In the dream, she was at Maggie's house. The two of them lying on Maggie's bed and giggling as the radio played and they flipped through magazines and pretended like they were sixteen instead of twelve. Old enough to drive. Old enough to go on dates and stop at the Dairy Queen on the way home from school when the weather was warm and get a Blizzard. All the freedoms a person could want.

Just be still, beautiful. You stay in that dream.

A woman's voice, breaking through the ethereal barrier between the dream version of Maggie's room and the real world.

Don't worry. Don't turn around. You'll be safe now. The woman spoke again, and Alexa wanted to ask, "Who are you?" but found when she did, it was Maggie who answered. "I'm Maggie, silly. You know, duh, your best friend?"

And Alexa's head swiveled from the dream version of her friend and up to the ceiling, as if she could see through the confines of her dream and discover who'd been speaking.

The radio played. Maggie turned more pages of the magazine.

And then, another voice broke through, one Alexa knew by heart. It played from the radio speakers in Maggie's room, staticky and not quite crisp. Her father's voice.

"No, no, no, no, no."

"Dad?" Alexa called out.

"*I'm sorry, I'm sorry, I'm sorry.*"

Alexa jumped off the bed and over to the radio sitting on Maggie's dresser. She leaned in close, putting her ear close to the speaker.

"*Okay, okay, okay! No more!*"

Something was happening to him. Was he dreaming, too?

"Wake up!" Alexa told herself. "Wake up!"

She had to see what was going on.

Sleep, beautiful. The woman's voice again, coming from above. *Not much longer now.*

And then, from the radio speakers, she heard her father begin to choke, then gag.

"He's getting sick!" Alexa's eyes bored into the radio. She reached for the volume knob and cranked it up, trying to hear more clearly what was happening out in the real word, outside her dream.

"Alexa, come look at this guy. I think I want to marry him. He's *gorgeous!*" Maggie called to her from the bed.

"Wake up!" Alexa shouted to herself.

More gagging from the radio speaker. Desperate gasps of air.

And just as the sympathy Alexa began to feel worked its way up from her heart—the sympathy any child will inherently feel for a parent in distress, a parent who might be struggling to stay alive—an image flashed in her head. An image that squashed the sympathy back down, mashed it to nothing.

Her father walking across the office and yanking her from the computer chair. Pulling her into a close hug, stroking her hair and telling her everything was okay. Gripping her tighter as she tried to pull away. Telling her she was beautiful. Beautiful, beautiful, beautiful.

More gagging from the radio, the sound of somebody

choking on soup, and then what sounded like a cat trying to cough up a hairball.

Her father's hands sliding down her shoulders. Down her torso. Reaching under her shirt. Beautiful, beautiful, beautiful. To her chest. Lingering there. Feeling. Exploring. Sighing. Moving lower. Finding the waistband of her pants. Slipping beneath it. Down, down, down. Finding what he was looking for.

And Alexa didn't want to wake up anymore.

She liked it in Maggie's room. She walked back to the bed and joined her friend and looked at the gorgeous guy who Maggie was going to marry.

On the radio, the music had started playing again.

When Alexa woke that morning, she knew her father was dead before she saw him. She'd opened her eyes and had seen the sun warming the motel room's wall, her own shadow enlarged, making her feel bigger than life.

She remembered everything—the woman's voice, the dream of Maggie's room, the choking, the gagging, and then the feeling of everything being over. Better. Renewed.

Safe.

She sat up in the bed and turned over. Saw her father's body with the empty pill bottle next to it. Saw his dried sick on his face and thought it to be such a wonderfully symbolic image. They'd learned about symbolism in English, and she was proud of herself for finding an application for it in real life.

She walked over to her father's body, looking down at him without sadness. She picked up the pill bottle and replaced the lid and then stuffed it into her pocket. A token that would remind her you might never truly know a person. Not even your own father.

"I guess the monsters won," Alexa said as she headed for the door, off to find somebody to tell. Off to start the rest of her life.

Or maybe you were the monster this whole time.

[21]

LANCE WALKED OUT MOTEL ROOM FIVE'S DOOR AND WAS suddenly pinned down with headlights of an approaching vehicle.

The sun was gone, day sneakily shifting into night once again with the blink of Lance's eyes. He stopped immediately, taking his time and getting his bearings after the transition. Looked to his right, just on instinct, to see if he might still be able to make out the fading memory of the young girl Alexa making her way to the office. But he saw nothing but a few stray cigarette butts and pine needles blowing across the walkway in the gentle breeze sweeping across the lot.

Lance looked ahead, toward the headlights. The Ford Explorer that had been parked in front of room five was gone, so Lance was either witnessing a different day, or ...

("*Don't call the police. Don't report this. We've got to get rid of him and never speak about it again.*")

Or Quinten and Murry had done what had been needed.

The cones of light plastered Lance against the motel's wall like a deer on the highway, freezing him in place. But any sense of panic Lance might have felt as the truck—it *was* a truck, he could see that now—approached him never surfaced. He'd begun to understand at least one of the rules of this experience he was living, and that was that he was completely unseen. More unobtrusive than even the proverbial fly on the wall.

Except ... the boy did *see me, didn't he? Felt me, my presence, at the very least.*

Lance found himself wishing he could somehow rewind this episode he was living, go back to that moment inside room five when Quinten had reached out for him. What would have happened if Lance had let him succeed? Would he have found himself coming into existence in this time and space? Filling in with color the way the fuzzy-television people had when Quinten had embraced them in Lance's dream. Would Murry have been able to see him? The girl?

Would Quinten and he be able to talk?

The last possibility alone was what had Lance kicking himself for chickening out and shying away from the boy's touch.

The truck was a battered black thing that looked every bit the role of what somebody like Murry might drive. Something that was meant to be taken off-road. Down to the stream or the lake for fishing. Up into the mountains for hunting. Hauling what needed to be hauled. Banged on and scratched up and used for its purpose without any care of vanity. A truck with history. A part of its owner. It began heading for the end of the motel, toward the office.

When it parked, the engine was cut off and Quinten opened the passenger door and stepped down. Even from where Lance was standing, he could see the contemplation in the boy's expression, and it was mixed with something else. Worry?

Lance began walking toward the truck, his footsteps quick. Quinten stepped up onto the walkway and stood, waiting. Murry emerged from the driver's side. He looked tired, defeated. All at once unhealthy. Quinten's eyes bored holes into his uncle, locked and loaded and ready to fire.

Murry's face, haggard and pleading, as if to say, *please, let's not do this*, looked to his nephew and waited.

"That was too easy," Quinten said, the words echoing off the motel's walls before getting swallowed by the surrounding trees.

Murry said nothing.

Quinten stepped forward, crossed his arms, then uncrossed them, then crossed them again. "Why?"

Murry shrugged, a pathetic sight that reminded Lance of a child when being scolded and asked to explain itself. "You said we had to get rid of him. What did you think we were going to do?"

"No," Quinten shook his head. "That's not what I'm asking. Why was it so easy?"

"I don't understand," Murry said. But Lance could tell he knew exactly what the boy was asking him.

"Murry, you knew exactly what you were doing tonight. The car, the body. You knew exactly where to go and exactly what do to. The best way to drive, the best time, everything was meticulous. Everything was so *planned*. How?"

Murry spoke louder now, more defensive. "You told me to come up with something good. I did as instructed. You told me to *trust you*. Well, how much more trust do you want from me than going along with your notion that we need to dump a body like some goddamn psycho criminal? And he was a cop! We could both go to jail, you know that, right? Both our lives could be over right this second. Think about your aunt. Think about your *mother*. How would *she* survive without you?"

Something about this last statement made Lance step closer to the two, positioning himself so his shins were nearly touching the truck's front bumper. He looked back and forth, from Quinten, to Murry, and then back to Quinten. Waiting. The line about Quinten's mother had sliced through the air, severing the conversation for a moment.

Quinten was quiet. Still. His eyes never leaving his uncle's. And then, he took a breath and his face morphed into something that might have been sympathy before he closed his eyes completely.

"Quinten?" Murry asked, taking a small step forward before stopping. "Are you alright?"

Lance looked at the boy. He looked like he was meditating. Focusing. Drifting away in his mind.

"Quinten!" Murry was rounding the truck now and Lance stepped back to avoid the contact. Murry reached out with both hands, making a move to grab the boy by the shoulders, but the boy moved first. His eyes shooting open and him taking a quick step back.

And they saw it. Both Murry and Lance saw the new knowledge carried in the boy's eyes.

"You've done this before," Quinten said.

Murry held up a hand. "Quinten, listen. I—"

"You've done this all before. That's how you were able to put it all together so quickly. You did the same thing with..." Quinten's voice cracked, suddenly overcome with emotion. He took a breath and swallowed. "You did it with the Backstroms."

Murry became angry. "Dammit, boy! Did you get in my head? Did you? We've talked about that! You can't just go poking around inside other peoples'—"

"Those kind, innocent people. You ... you *murdered* them."

Murry took a step toward his nephew. "Quinten, you don't understand. Just listen to me! It wasn't like that. They—"

"They what, Murry? What could they have possibly done to make you shoot them?"

The boy was speaking softly, but Lance could feel the anger, the disappointment radiating from Quinten's body.

Murry's eyes softened. He sighed and his head dropped down, and when he spoke he was barely audible. "They didn't do anything. It wasn't about what they did. It was about what they might do."

Quinten shook his head. "That only makes it worse."

"We were only trying to protect you."

At this, Quinten looked to the motel office door. He threw his head back and groaned. "Of course. She didn't listen to a word I said. Didn't trust me." He looked back to his uncle. "I suppose it's not entirely your fault. I'm to blame, too. I should have never told you two what I am. What I can do. I should have never asked you to shoulder that burden with me."

"You're our nephew, Quinten. Hell, you're like our *son*. You know that."

"I do." Quinten nodded. "Which is why this is going to be so hard."

And then the boy turned and started to walk across the parking lot, headed for the road.

"Quinten, where are you going?" Murry took a few steps after his nephew. "Quinten?"

The boy said nothing. Kept walking.

"Quinten, are you going to the police? You don't have to. I'll turn myself in! Keep yourself and your aunt out of it!" Murry's voice faded into the night.

Quinten walked into the road and made a right, continuing on, disappearing behind the tree line. Leaving them. He never looked back. Lance watched him go, watched Murry stand in the parking lot shaking his head and pleading under his breath, and when the man turned around, Lance saw the tears in his eyes.

"*Shit.*" Murry headed for the office. His head hung low, the

177

feeling of some monumental change permeating the air. A page turning. One story ending, another beginning.

Murry slipped into the office and Lance moved to follow. He sucked in a breath and prepared himself and walked through the office door and—

And he was back outside. Standing on the concrete walkway just before reaching room six.

There was snow on the ground, a fierce cold in the air. A bitter chill that sank deep into your bones. The snow was still falling, hard and fast, just as it'd been when Lance had arrived at the motel.

But another coldness sank even deeper inside Lance. An icy grip on his heart, a surge of fear in his veins that made his head light and his vision wobble.

Parked just in front of room six was an orange-and-white Volkswagen bus, partially covered in snow.

[22]

(1993)

Quinten pulled his beanie down over his ears and then pulled on his gloves. The weather had gotten bad, temperatures plummeting overnight and the fear of a massive snowstorm being instilled in the town's residents by enthusiastic meteorologists. It was supposed to roll in later this evening, once the sun had set. He'd probably have to walk home in it, so he wore his boots instead of sneakers, heavy rubber things Murry had gotten him one year for his birthday.

"Can't beat a good pair of boots," his uncle had said as Quinten had unwrapped them. "Protect your feet, protect the body."

Quinten had been grateful for the gift. He'd been grateful for everything his aunt and uncle had given him over the years.

He walked softly down the hall and peeked inside his mother's bedroom, found what he'd expected, which was her sprawled out across the mattress asleep with the television on too loud and an ashtray overflowing with cigarette butts on the nightstand.

He went inside and switched the television off. "I'm headed to work, Mom. I'll bring home some dinner, but try and eat lunch. There's deli meat in the fridge." His mother made no indication that she'd heard him. Which he'd also expected, and was why earlier he'd written out this exact phrase on a scrap of paper and taped it to the front of the fridge.

Quinten stepped out and closed his mother's bedroom door and made his way to the front of the townhouse. He stepped out onto the front stoop, closing the door softly and locking it behind him. He looked at the sky, which was gray and boring. Breathed in the air, which was icy cold and smelled faintly of pine. Closed his eyes. Breathed in again. Shivered.

He opened his eyes. He'd felt something. Nothing tangible, but a trace of something different lurking in the air, a little ways off now, but heading his way. It could be anything, he told himself. It could be nothing at all. But instinct and experience worked hard to dispel this rationalization. He shrugged to himself. He'd known it was coming, had for some time now, the last year or so at least. But the realization of today possibly being the day sat heavy on his heart. He knew he might not make it. In fact, it almost seemed certain that he would not. The stars had their plans, and his role might have come to its end. His purpose fulfilled. He wouldn't question it. It would do no good to do so. He'd learned this much, if nothing else, over these last seventeen years of being a soldier for the light.

Quinten took the three concrete steps down to the sidewalk and stopped, looked to his right, to where the street would end and then he could make another right and find himself walking out of town and into the county, only two miles from his aunt and uncle's motel.

He went left instead. Headed into town to the coffee shop,

where he would work in the morning before eating a quick lunch and then walking the three blocks to the Pizza Hut, where he waited tables and made decent tips and got to bring home a pie for dinner most nights if he wanted to. He stayed busy, *kept* himself busy on purpose. The busier he was, the less time he had to think about everything else.

He missed them, his aunt and uncle. It was simple as that. From an early age, they'd essentially raised him off and on as his mother had battled her addictions. She'd attempted to repay them—literally—the best she could after the accident. And while they'd accepted, starting the motel which had been somewhat of a dream for the two of them, Quinten knew that no amount of money would ever compensate them for all they'd done for him. They'd given him a life, a childhood his mother would have been absent for, and guidance as he'd become a young adult.

And they'd kept his secrets. All these years, they'd harbored the knowledge of what made him special and not spoken a word of it to anyone. They'd done all they could to protect him from being exposed and all the downfall that would potentially follow. They knew that he would never live a normal life, but they'd tried hard to give him one. They'd given him chores, given him a job, given him a home away from home. He'd loved them so much for that.

And then they'd gone too far.

Quinten walked down the sidewalk, kicking pebbles as he went, shaking his head for the millionth time as he considered it all again.

The thing that made him the saddest was that if today was the day, he might never see them again, and the last emotions he'd shared with them were anger and regret.

He hadn't spoken to his aunt or uncle in months, not since the night during the summer when he'd learned the truth about the Backstroms, the nice young couple who he'd helped, the ones who'd been haunted, for lack of a better word, by the ghost of the man's mother. Quinten had spoken with her in the way only he could, wordless conversations taking place in the ether while he'd held real conversations with real words with the Backstroms as they ate lunch together in the diner. She'd been stubborn, the ghost of the man's mother. Rude, if Quinten was being completely honest. But in the end, he'd accomplished what he'd needed to, helping her to let go and say goodbye to her son, and then move on to where she belonged.

She'd loved the man very much, and while Quinten could feel it, he hoped the man had also been able to feel some trace of it, too. That he wouldn't spend the rest of his life convinced his mother cared nothing for him.

The rest of his life...

How short that had ended up being.

Because later that night, in an ironic twist of fate, Quinten's uncle had killed both the man and his wife. Shot them dead. The man first, as he'd lunged for Murry, attempting to thwart the attack, and then the woman, who'd frozen in shock at the sight of her husband's dying body.

Quinten had seen all this, pulling the images from his uncle's memories. Finding himself nearly freezing in shock as well, unable to believe what he was seeing. But the anger and disappointment and regret had quickly risen up, erasing the shock.

Everything had changed.

And they would never recover from it.

His uncle had not denied what Quinten had seen, knowing perfectly well what Quinten was capable of. Instead, he'd offered up a defense of trying to keep Quinten safe, saying that the Backstroms could mean trouble for him. That night after he'd walked home, Aunt Meriam had confirmed this on the phone while Quinten had stood in his and his mother's kitchen with the telephone handset held loosely in his grip. She told Quinten what she'd overheard. She had even tried to take the blame, saying the entire stunt had been her idea from the start.

"Nobody was supposed to actually get hurt," she'd said.

But whatever the reason, whatever was supposed to have happened, two innocent people had ended up dead. And Quinten knew exactly whose fault it all was.

His.

If he hadn't confided in his aunt and uncle about the full extent of his abilities, the Backstroms would still be alive.

If he wasn't who he was, lives would not have been lost.

That night during the summer in the motel's parking lot had taught Quinten an important lesson. He needed to be alone for the rest of his life. No good would come from keeping anyone close to him. Anybody who knew his secrets instantly became a liability, both to themselves and to him.

He would never again make the same mistake he'd made with his aunt and uncle.

From now on, it was only him.

After the brief phone call with Meriam after he'd walked home that night, he found he couldn't hold still, his mind too wound up. He left, wandering the city blocks, his mind drifting across clouds of time, recapping all the decisions he'd made, all the moments of his life that had somehow led him to right then, with the fresh knowledge that his uncle had committed murder, and unsure what exactly to do about it.

The answer had finally come to him sometime before the sun began to rise.

Murry and Meriam had kept Quinten's secret all these years, so now it was his turn to keep theirs. But there was a personal stipulation to this solo agreement, a nonnegotiable clause that was meant to protect them all.

Quinten would never speak to them again.

They might not understand, but they didn't need to.

Because by then, Quinten had already known that the end was coming.

He made it to the coffee shop and pushed through the door, greeted by the smell of freshly ground beans and warm pastries. Familiar sights and scents and sounds that pushed out all the negative thoughts in his mind and replaced them with the routines of his workday.

The shift went by quickly, a steady crowd of people rotating in and out, getting their caffeine fixes and satisfying their carb cravings.

Quinten ate lunch and then walked the three blocks to Pizza Hut, where the dinner rush had been cut off a little earlier than usual because of the snow that had started to fall, but he still managed to end the night with an above-average tip total. He wasn't scheduled to close, but he stuck around anyway, helping the kitchen staff shut things down before he headed out, stepping out into the restaurant's parking lot, carrying a large sausage and mushroom pizza in his arms, ready for the walk home.

The snow was coming down hard, a good three inches of the stuff already on the ground, crisscrossed with tire tracks of the cars that had already come and gone for their dinner. Quinten stepped off the sidewalk and headed across the lot, sinking into the snow and silently thanking his uncle again for the boots.

The town was mostly deserted. Several businesses had closed early, fearing the worst from the impending storm. The white of snow illuminated everything—the road, the sidewalk, the clock in the center of town, the tops of buildings. Everything looked bright and clean and pristine. The phrase *winter wonderland* came to mind, and Quinten imagined a dancing team of snowmen doing the Soft Shoe or the Charleston across the city's center square. He wished it was closer to Christmas, so the city would have already strung up all the lights and hung the wreaths and put out the decorations in the park. It would have looked spectacular tonight. All of it.

And it was so quiet. With no people and no cars, each and every one of his own footsteps crunching though the snow seemed to reverberate through the town. He felt like the only person left on Earth, and for a brief moment he allowed himself to indulge in this fantasy, wondering how different it would be if he didn't have to keep everything that he was a secret.

Which he knew was just a metaphor for wondering what it would be like to be a normal teenage boy. Someone whose only cares were dating and sports and GPAs and parties and Nintendo. He didn't often let himself go down this road, knowing it would only end in frustration and sadness. But something about tonight told him it was okay. Tonight, for these few remaining moments of his walk home, alone in the quiet and blinding white sparkle of the town, he could be whoever he wanted to be. Could live however he wanted to live. This was his moment.

Right now, he was free.

Ten minutes later, he turned left onto his and his mother's street. Snow-covered cars lined the sidewalk in front of the row of townhouses like sleeping guard dogs. The streetlamps cast glowing cones of snowfall across the road. The porchlights twinkled like stars.

It was all beautiful.

Quinten walked right down the middle of the street, clinging on to his moment of freedom. Knowing that as soon as he climbed the steps up to his home's door, unlocked the deadbolt and went inside, the feeling would vanish. Washed away by real life.

The feeling ended up vanishing much sooner.

He was halfway down the road when he heard the sound of the engine behind him, turning onto the street, followed by headlights growing in intensity, throwing his shadow far in front of him.

And Quinten knew. All of him, every fiber of his mind and body and soul came to life, alerting him, solidifying the thought that had been floating in the periphery of his mind all day.

Today was the day.

He turned around slowly, standing his ground in the middle of the road as the headlights blinded him and the sound of the engine grew louder.

And he felt it. A force of energy accompanying the headlights and the engine. A powerful source of darkness, stronger than anything he'd ever experienced, coming straight for him. Closer and closer.

Tires squished through the snow and then brakes engaged and the vehicle slowed, skidding a bit before finally coming to a complete stop a few feet away from him. Quinten stood, holding his pizza in his hands, staring into the face of an orange-and-white Volkswagen bus.

Run. Move. Do something!

The instinctive part of his brain screamed at him. Fight or flight. Survive. *Live.*

But Quinten stayed put. Waited. The obedient soldier. This was it. His moment. The next step in the stars' plan. The end of his purpose. One last task.

Because the other one was out there now. The one who Quinten had felt come into existence in a way that could only be described as being present for the creation of a new star in the Universe. A shift in the entire balance of everything. The one.

And this last mission of Quinten's was simple: Whatever

little knowledge he had about the one, don't let the darkness have it. No matter the cost.

The passenger door of the Volkswagen bus opened, squeaky hinges echoing off the buildings. A man stepped out, tall and thin and dressed in black.

He moved carefully through the snow, stepping around the door and coming closer. Quinten saw that the black outfit was actually the outfit of a priest—*a cassock*, he thought. *It's called a cassock.*

But Quinten knew this man was not a man of God. He was, in fact, as far from it as possible.

The man offered a small smile. "Quinten, hello."

Quinten said nothing.

Had to nearly step back at the force of Evil coming from the man before him.

"My partner and I thought you might like to go for a ride."

Quinten said nothing. Frozen not in indecision, but suddenly in fear. Was he ready to die? Was he *willing* to die? Die for a person whom he'd never even met?

He looked away from the man, glancing over his shoulder and taking one last look at the front door to his home.

Mom...

"There's no need to involve your mother in this," the man said. "But that's up to you." He'd sounded completely passive, but the threat lingered in the air.

Quinten looked back to the man, met his eyes. Looked into them for a long time. Thinking. Deciding. Wondering at all the possibilities of both the past and the present.

A minute later, the road was empty, tire tracks heading toward the town's limits, an uneaten pizza discarded in the street, the box growing soggy in the snow.

The Reverend sat still and straight in the Volkswagen's passenger seat, staring ahead through the windshield and the falling snow as the headlights cut their path. He looked over to his partner who was driving and said, "Just another half mile or so, up on the left."

The Surfer nodded, not saying a word. Not needing to. He gave a brief whip of his head, tossing a bit of his long blond hair out of his face, and then eased on the brakes, slowing the bus, wanting to be cautious. Wanting to avoid sliding off the road and into a tree or flipping over and then rolling end over end over end. Not so much for his safety. No, he'd be just fine. For the boy's protection. He was precious cargo. The Surfer assumed the boy would die—would prefer it, in fact; it had been some time since he'd been in the presence of death and he was beginning to crave it—but they needed him alive for a bit longer. Until they got what they'd been sent for.

"There," the Reverend said, pointing ahead. "See the lights?"

The motel was small, only six rooms and an office. Perfectly secluded. No other cars in the parking lot. And nobody would be coming by. Not on a night like this. Not this late and with the snow falling and the temperatures dropping. The Reverend had pulled the motel from the boy's mind. Dug through his memories quickly while they'd stood face-to-face in the snow in the middle of the road. What a wonderfully convenient place to discover it had been. The image of the motel—and its two owners—had been filed away near the front of the boy's active thoughts, a place he loved. People he loved. And now, ironically, the Reverend thought, it would be the place where the boy would end. But maybe they were doing the boy a favor in that regard. Because wouldn't a person prefer to die in a place they could call home, instead of someplace foreign to them?

The Reverend could only suppose this sort of thought. It

had been some time since he'd fully understood a human's range of emotions. He turned around in his seat, looked at the boy in the back, sitting like a perfect little captive. His eyes were closed and he was breathing deeply, almost as if he were sleeping. He'd put up no fight. Offered no resistance.

And he'd said nothing.

But that would change very soon.

"Park at the end. The last room," the Reverend said.

The Surfer obeyed.

In the backseat of the bus, Quinten was working hard. He was building. Constructing walls in his mind. Towering walls that wrapped around his thoughts, secured his memories from outside threats. Wall after wall after wall. Thick and deeply layered. His mind spun, his brain working at dizzying speed. Despite the cold, there was sweat on his brow.

He'd felt the man in the priest's garb poking around in his thoughts while they'd been in the road outside his townhouse, and Quinten knew exactly what he had to do. He could not escape them, could not fight them physically. But he now understood his objective was protection. Protection of any information about the one.

He had little. Almost none, in fact. But any help to the darkness was too much. Any shred of knowledge that might lead them to the one and keep him from carrying out his purpose, from being the salvation the world needed, was Quinten's responsibility to protect. And protect it he would. With all his strength and might and power.

Tonight, he would fall. But the darkness would not win.

[23]

Lance stood frozen as the snow flurries whipped around him in the wind. He stared at the orange-and-white Volkswagen bus, flashes of memory of that night exploding like flash bulbs in his mind—the night his mother had sacrificed herself and propelled Lance on this journey. The night she had been murdered.

After the initial rush of fear had subsided enough for the paralysis to break, Lance's first instinct was to turn and run. Head for the woods and get as far away as possible from the vehicle that surely had ushered along with it the cause of all Lance's pain and anger and hatred. The two who had changed everything. The two who hunted him.

The Reverend and the Surfer. Nameless entities, soldiers for the opposing army. *Creatures.* Because Lance knew now, after what had happened in Sugar Beach, that the Surfer's abilities were far beyond the world of humans and mortal beings. The Reverend ... he was still somewhat of a mystery, but his dark powers were unmistakable. Not to be taken lightly. Lance had gotten lucky before and...

Before.

Sugar Beach.

Lance took a breath and calmed himself and tried to ratio-nalize. Remembered that at this very moment, he was no longer viewing the present. Not seeing current events. The image of the orange-and-white Volkswagen bus was not something tangible directly in front of him, but something like a projection, a recreated memory of the Universe. Just like everything else Lance had witnessed since he'd stepped across the threshold of his motel room. It was part of a story he was meant to see. A clue in the mystery he was being forced to live through.

And something—instinct, intuition, gifts, abilities, take your pick—was tapping Lance on the temple and saying, *This is it. This is why you're here.*

Everything. The past, the present, and somehow the future, all seemed to culminate right here in front of this motel room. A grand collision for which he was responsible.

But why? What was he—

Lance gasped, sucked in a sharp breath and let it out with a cry, doubling over and clutching his head. Searing pain had shot through his mind, like a bolt of lightning across the sky. No, that was too quick. It had been more like a blowtorch, a hot, explo-sive flame charring a path across the horizon of his thoughts. Burning away, working to remove something. To destroy.

Again.

This time, Lance went down on one knee, his hands viselike on either side of his skull as another blast of heat tore through. A buzz saw of pain grinding, slicing through with sparks flying.

But this time, something different. This time, in that moment when the pain had struck, Lance had felt ... like he wasn't himself. Not in the sense one usually uses such a phrase —like when they act out of character or are feeling a bit under the weather—but in the truest sense the words could possibly be interpreted. A momentary transition of consciousness. His mind

—his active thoughts and all his memories—was not his own. Lance existed not as Lance, but as somebody else.

In that moment, that brief flash of agony, Lance had become the boy—Quinten.

And Lance had seen it all. Not the boy's entire life, his past, but Lance had learned the cause of the pain.

They had him. The Reverend and Surfer had Quinten right inside room six, right here and now, and they were ripping apart his mind. Searching. Tearing apart the boy's defenses, sifting through the rubble and trying to locate—

"Me."

Lance said it aloud, and though he didn't understand, couldn't fathom, how Quinten could have known about him in whatever year Lance was witnessing, he accepted this truth completely. The Reverend and the Surfer's pursuit of Lance had started long, long ago. And they'd been ruthless in their efforts from the very beginning.

Quinten was suffering because of him.

How many people had suffered, how many had *died* because of Lance Brody?

Why did he deserve to live and they did not?

Lance felt anger begin to boil. Anger mixed with such confusion, a melting pot of unanswered questions. *He* would kill just to be able to ask, *Why? Why me?*

But right now, he had to save the boy. They were in the room only a few feet away, the Reverend and the Surfer. Lance didn't know what powers they would have against him in the state he existed in. Didn't know if the Surfer could see him in the future the way Lance would see him in the past.

Lance had gotten rid of them—with the help of some friends —on the shore of Sugar Beach. Temporarily, at least. Because Lance was under no delusion that they would be gone for good. Would not allow himself that sense of peace. Because even if not them, there would likely be others. Others who would pick up the trail and start where the Reverend and the Surfer had left off.

But for now, Lance chose to believe that the two were temporarily nonexistent in the present, in the modern day in which, somewhere, Lance Brody was living and breathing. He hoped that whatever barrier existed between the present and the past would be enough protection.

Lance regained his footing, standing upright again and staring at the orange-and-white Volkswagen bus while his thoughts slowed and he prepared himself for what he had to do. The boy needed him, and he would not let him down. Quinten was suffering because of Lance, and Lance would do all he could to make it end.

Lance was about to turn around, head for the door to room six, when the strongest feeling of déjà vu pushed away all other thoughts. His eyes slid across the Volkswagen bus from the front to the back, and then out across the snow-covered parking lot until his focus reached the road, empty and quiet and lonely-looking with the clouded night sky stretching far and away. He searched for sights of the familiar, trying to reconcile why the feeling that he'd seen this all before—had *lived* this all before—had hit him with such force.

And then his eyes fell on a particular spot on the road, just across the threshold of the parking lot. The pieces snapped together to complete the puzzle. The circle completed.

He *had* seen this all before. The Volkswagen bus hadn't been part of it, hidden, for some reason, the other time, but the scene playing out with Lance standing in front of room six, about to make his entry, had already burned a place into Lance's memories.

He'd seen it all from the other side, as the other *him*. Lance of the present and not Lance witnessing the past.

Lance looked directly at the spot in the road where he knew he'd stood in the dream he'd had, where he'd witnessed the boy and fuzzy-television people and then watched himself turn to enter room six before he'd jolted awake and had started this unfathomable mission that, up until this point, had not had a clear objective. He marveled at how, right here and now, though he felt completely in control of his mind and body, free will driving his every action, on some level, this had all been predetermined.

In a gesture that felt so out-of-body, so foreign and unnatural, Lance raised a hand and waved to the spot on the road where he'd stood. Waved to himself in another dimension.

He wondered, just like he had when he'd witnessed the action before, if it truly was a wave of goodbye.

Then he turned his back on the part of him that existed on the road and moved to open the door to room six.

24

LANCE STOOD BEFORE THE DOOR TO ROOM SIX, AND JUST AS he moved to step forward and allow himself to be transported through it, a quick flash of worry struck.

How can I fight them? How can I help Quinten when I have no physical presence here?

He'd been so worked up after seeing the Volkswagen bus and then getting the look inside Quinten's head as the Reverend and Surfer tortured the boy's mind, Lance hadn't stopped to think what his plan of action might be.

But I do have a presence, he thought then, remembering that moment inside room five after the young girl had left and Quinten had suddenly fixed his eyes on the exact spot Lance where had been standing before, then reached out for him. *It might not be much, but if he could see me, maybe they can too.*

And if they could see him, maybe they could feel him. Maybe he could impact whatever was happening enough to attempt to stop it.

But if that were true, if he could find a way to interact with the people and objects in the past, did that also mean they could interact with him? Touch him? Hurt him?

Only one way to find out.

Lance gathered his courage and stepped forward, into the door. But he went nowhere. Instead of the normal rush of speed and blurred vision that usually accompanied his moments of teleportation from one side of a door to another, this time when Lance reached the door and took the last step to move through it, it was if he'd walked into a *real* door. One made of heavy wood or metal, locked and solid and unforgiving. He'd struck the object with too much force and then literally bounced off it. There'd been no pain, which was good, just a quick buzz and then the connection with something solid, a faint vibration through his entire self as he'd been flung backward.

And Lance might have been able to accept the fact that he'd walked into an actual door, that the past was somehow solidifying itself, morphing from vision to tangible objects, if it hadn't been for what he'd really seen as he'd struck the door.

The impact had not come as Lance had initially made contact with the vision of the door. No, he'd seen and felt himself begin to move through it, had seen the rest of the world begin to blur and fade away, had heard the rush of speed far off, coming for him to take him away. He *had* started to move through it, but something on the other side had stopped him.

Lance knew exactly what was happening.

They're protecting themselves. They've put up some sort of defense. I should have known.

And while Lance willingly accepted this fact, another thought came with it. *Do they already know I'm here? Do they— in the past—even know who I am yet? Could they capture me in this existence, instead of having to do it again in the future?*

The time-travel-metaphysical-dream-world-vision-filled riddle was starting to hurt his head.

And then another blast of heat shot through his skull, another glimpse of a wall being knocked down by the wrecking ball that was the Surfer in the boy's mind. Lance grunted in pain and was fueled by it. Like a starter's pistol going off in his soul, the jolt of electricity had at once changed him. Primed him.

He found himself completely consumed by anger. *Rage* pulsed through him in such a force that he wasn't sure he'd ever experienced before. His lungs felt full of something other than air, full of power, full of energy. Full of...

Salvation.

The word danced across his consciousness. Not his own voice, but the voice of another. A voice dwindling with each passing moment.

Lance ran straight for the door, his fists clenched and his shoulder lowered. He charged like a bull, ready to knock over the entire motel if that was what it came to. He closed his eyes and grunted in frustration and made one final push with his legs and hit the door. It exploded inward, the door frame splintering and cracking. And Lance tumbled two steps inside before he stopped himself. He managed to catch his balance and stand upright, his vision clearing and the realization that he'd succeeded spiking adrenaline through his veins.

"Who's there?" It was the Reverend, standing in front of the bed against the room's far wall. At the sight of him, Lance flushed with fresh anger. He clenched and unclenched his fists, feeling that anger grow inside him, feeling the energy he was generating with it.

The Reverend looked angry, his eyes narrowing to slits and his mouth pursing into a sour-looking worm, as if asking who dared to have the gall to interrupt them.

He took a step forward, eyes searching the doorway, and Lance knew that the Reverend could not see him.

But the Surfer...

The Surfer, who'd been standing in front of the first bed, his board shorts and cut-off t-shirt looking as tattered and frayed as ever, his long hair not in a ponytail but hanging in splayed fingers down across his face, raised a hand and grabbed ahold of the Reverend's shoulder as the man had headed for the opened door—headed for Lance.

The Reverend stopped, turned and looked back to the Surfer, asking, "What? What is it?" before taking a step backward and refocusing on the opened doorway.

And that was when Lance felt the first chill of fear begin to weasel its way in again, digging a small hole into his armor of anger and energy and resolution. The Surfer squinted, reaching up and pushing the hair out of his face—*Out of its face*, Lance corrected himself. For the Surfer was no man, no matter what his appearance might otherwise say. The Surfer's gaze locked onto Lance, clearly seeing through whatever veil existed between Lance's world and the present time.

And though the fear was gnawing its way in further, Lance stayed calm. Focused his energy on the things he could control—himself. He needed to test his situation, verify that the Surfer could actually see him. So, he started to walk, taking slow, sideways steps away from the door and across the room. Four long strides until he was right in front of the television stand, directly in between the Reverend and the Surfer.

The Surfer's eyes had followed him the entire way. He was still staring directly at Lance, but his eyes still remained squinted, and Lance would swear that for a moment or two the Surfer had lost him as Lance had worked his way across the room.

He can see me, but not clearly.

Just like the boy had in room five.

The boy...

Lance had been so focused on the Reverend and the Surfer as he'd crashed into the room that he'd not even noticed Quinten. The lights in the room had been off, the snowy white from the outdoors and the overhead lights from the overhang now stretched inside the opened door, giving everything it could touch a cold glow. And now Lance could see him, behind the Reverend and the Surfer, tied to a chair with duct tape, sitting alone in the shadows beside the first bed, his head hung down so that his chin was resting on his chest, his breathing irregular, his body soaked with sweat. Quinten.

And Lance felt the anger begin to swell again. Experienced such hatred for the two monsters before him. They'd killed his mother, a good woman—the *best* woman, a saint. The person he'd loved more than anything. And now they were going to kill this boy, a boy like Lance, a boy with gifts and abilities beyond the measure of the mortal world, a boy who, like Lance, had done and would hopefully continue doing such great things. Things for those who were hurting, those who were lost and sad, those who needed help in ways nobody but them even knew about. Lance had already seen this—the Backstroms, and the girl, Alexa, from room five—had seen and now understood why the Universe had brought him here, taken him on this trip through the past, to witness all the good that the boy stood for. And to let Lance know that he was not alone.

And right now, it was Lance's job to let the boy know that he wasn't alone either.

He would not let Quinten die like this, not at the hands of these monsters. Not today.

These thoughts swirled in Lance's mind, mixing with his rage, bonding with his anger, pulling in all the energy he could absorb. Lance breathed in deep, opened his eyes, which he'd not even remembered closing, and was stunned at what he saw. He was glowing, a faint red light emanating directly from his pores. But, no, that wasn't right. He stepped back and saw that it wasn't he that was actually glowing, but that he was cocooned in some sort of force field, a translucent ball of light, pulsing red with each beat of his heart.

The Surfer stared where Lance stood. The Reverend's eyes darted back and forth from his partner's face to where the Surfer was looking.

Lance stared back, feeling strange, feeling an odd sense of out-of-body power that he wasn't sure what do with, how to control. Growing, growing, growing. The red light getting bright and brighter and brighter.

And then Lance heard laughter. A foreign sound that sliced through the atmosphere of the room. The Reverend and Surfer turned in their spot, toward the source of the sound. Lance's eyes fixed on Quinten.

The boy was sitting upright, his eyes wide and looking straight at Lance with clarity that must have taken all the energy the boy had left. Lance could *feel* it, could feel the exhaustion in the boy's mind and body.

"He's ... here," Quinten said.

And Lance felt something new. Something like satisfaction and relief coming from the boy's mind.

The Surfer must have sensed it too, because he turned back quickly, staring back to where Lance was standing, looking like he wanted to do something, *needed* to act, but wasn't sure what or how. The Reverend took a step closer to the boy, leaning in and asking, "Who?"

And Lance thought he heard genuine concern in the Reverend's voice. A sound that was as sweet as anything Lance had ever heard.

"Salvation," the boy said.

Quinten said the word, and Lance recognized it as the same word he'd heard in his head when he'd been outside the room, preparing himself to make his move. He hadn't known what it had meant then, and he wasn't entirely sure he knew what it meant now, but when the boy had spoken, Lance had felt something inside of himself, a direct line of communication somehow created between him and Quinten, a secret tunnel through which they could pass their messages.

Salvation, the boy had said out loud. But what Lance had heard in his own mind was, *Hello, friend. Do it now.*

And suddenly there was clarity. Lance felt himself let out the deepest of breaths, a breath not from his lungs, but from his entire being. An expulsion of energy that had been pent up inside, somewhere deep down, growing in intensity and threatening to explode.

So Lance released it. Set it free.

The red glow surrounding him erupted in a million different directions, a bomb of energy that concussed the room in a shockwave of destruction. Both the Revered and the Surfer were thrown across the room, as if the engine of a massive jet had suddenly sparked to life and they'd been directly behind it. Their bodies flew through the air and struck the wall before falling down onto the bed and tumbling to the floor. The framed artwork fell from the wall, crashing to the carpet. The bedspreads and sheets flew up and off the bed, billowing and dancing in the waves of energy like they'd been caught in a tornado, pulled and tugged this way and that, whipping back and forth. The drawers of the nightstand emptied themselves onto the floor, a small black Bible flipping open, its pages shuffling as if being turned by the hands of the Holy Spirit. The lampshade of the bedside light simply folded in on itself, collapsing like a crushed paper cup, the bulb exploding beneath. The television screen shattered, raining bits of glass and plastic around Lance's feet.

And then the windows blew out, shards of glass mixing in with the wind and snow in the parking lot, sparkling in the air.

"Let's go!" It was the Reverend, running past Lance and heading for the opened door. "We have enough for now!"

The Surfer was standing again, between the two beds, seemingly oblivious to the destruction that occurred all around him. He was staring straight at Lance, and Lance could feel the Surfer's eyes sending their message. As if he were silently letting Lance know that he would remember this, that they would meet again. And then he left, his rubber flip-flops crunching the shattered glass around Lance's feet as he passed by, heading out the door to join the Reverend.

And then Lance felt something let go, like some mighty hand had been holding him in place all this time and he'd been completely unaware, and now a great weight lifted from his shoulders. He could *move* again, but as he took his first step, meaning to follow the Surfer out the door, it was as though he were slogging through quicksand, his feet like cement blocks he was dragging along.

He was completely exhausted. His mind, his body, and even his soul felt completely drained. It was a sense of depletion the likes of which he'd never experienced before, nor could he fully articulate. And then, a terrifying thought: *What if I'm dying? What if this is what death feels like?*

He managed to get himself to the door and then step outside, all in what seemed like slow motion, like everything was stuck in honey and he was trying to dig himself out. The rush of wind and the cold snow bit at him but did nothing to wake him, to energize him. There were tire tracks in the snow, and at the edge of the parking lot, he saw the taillights of the Volkswagen bus disappear around the bend. Gone.

Quinten, Lance remembered and made the laborious turn to go back inside, to rescue the only person he'd ever met who was just like him. He lifted one cement-block foot and stepped over the threshold, and then the other, and then—

A rush of speed. His vision blackening to nothing. A momentary feeling of weightlessness.

And then his eyes opened and Lance found himself sitting on the floor of his motel room.

It was over.

He was back to the present.

25

LANCE SAT ON THE FLOOR, THE CARPET FEELING STALE AND sticky beneath his palms, his head drifting slowly back to full consciousness, the room coming into focus, as if he'd just awakened from a long midday nap. He felt groggy, his head full of fluff. He took three big breaths of air and closed his eyes tight. Counted to ten and reopened them. Felt himself sloughing off the remainder of the past and brining himself back to the present. Felt the exhaustion that had crippled him while he'd been in room six begin to fade, his energy restoring itself like a gas tank at the pump.

He looked around the room and saw his cell phone lying on the table, still tethered to the charging cord that snaked down and into the wall receptacle. He saw his backpack—his trusty traveling companion—exactly where he'd left it on the bed. Saw the dust on the pictures hanging on the wall and the chips and scratches on the headboards.

Yes, he thought he was definitely back to his real life.

But, there was one final test.

Lance stood, slowly, his head swimming a bit and his legs wobbling at first before he reclaimed control of his muscles and was able to walk forward toward the door. A foot away, he reached out his hand and pressed his palm against the wood. He made contact and had never been happier to actually feel the resistance of a door against his touch.

The world was real and he was alive in it.

He reached down and grabbed the handle and turned it, taking gleeful satisfaction as he swung the door open. He stepped outside and shivered at the chill, quickly pulling up his hood. The wind was dying down and the snow that was still falling was now doing so in a lazy flutter from the sky instead of the torrent of fury from before. He looked to his left, eyeing room six, was blasted with the memory of what had happened. Having so many questions about what he'd done—what he'd been *able* to do. Questions that maybe only one person could possibly answer.

Quinten.

And what had happened to the boy? Lance had kept the Reverend and Surfer from inflicting any further harm to Quinten, but when he'd gone back to help, to try and speak with him —whether out loud or through the secret tunnel they had somehow constructed between them,

(*Hello, friend. Do it now.*)

Lance had been whisked away, thrown back to now. Here.

Meriam!

Lance spun around and looked back through his motel room's opened door and saw the phone sitting on the nightstand. *How long has it been?* he wondered. How many hours had passed since he'd made the phone call and called Meriam a liar and told her that he knew about the letter the dead woman had left her? How much time since they'd agreed to talk and both of them lay their cards on the table? Was it too late?

No, it couldn't be. If Lance had to break down the door and wake her from sleep and prop her up in a chair himself, he would. He had to know. Had to know what had happened to Quinten and where to find him. This was one of the biggest moments—if not *the* biggest moment—of his life and he wasn't going to let anything get in his way. Not after all he'd been through. All he'd lost.

After all he'd done for others, he was taking this for himself.

He rushed across the room and grabbed the phone from its cradle, punching the number for the office. It rang twice before Meriam answered, "Yes?"

She sounded mildly irritated.

"It's me," Lance said. "I got held up," he offered. "I'm still coming over, and we're still talking about this."

Silence from the other end of the line. Seconds that grew and grew. Finally, Meriam said, "You just called me, maybe a minute or two ago. The coffee hasn't even finished brewing yet."

Lance hung up the phone. He wasn't even going to attempt to explain. Because how could he explain something he didn't understand?

Like his entire life.

The Universe had allowed him to spend hours, witness several days spread over who knows how long a timeframe, all within a couple of minutes in Lance's reality. It was revelatory moments like this one that caused Lance to wonder if he'd ever had any control over any of his life at all, or if it was all just some predetermined path he was being led along under the guise of having free will.

In the end, he figured it had to be a little of both, because the former option was too overwhelming to process, too depressing to accept as the truth.

He thought about Leah. Lance had made the painful decision to leave her behind in Westhaven, doing what he thought he knew deep down to be the right thing. Wanting to protect her. But now, she had made her own decision, regardless of his.

She was leaving her home and coming to him. They would join together again soon, and what happened after that ... they'd just have to figure out as they went along.

Or so Lance had thought.

Because in moments like this one, he had to ask himself: Was Leah's decision to join him her own, or had there been a gentle nudge from the Universe involved. Had Lance made the wrong decision in Westhaven and now the higher powers were working to correct it?

Lance couldn't dwell on these types of things for long. There were some mysteries that even he, with all his abilities, simply could not solve. Instead, he chose to live one day at a time. The way everyone should. Each moment an opportunity that should not be passed on.

He cinched his hoodie's drawstrings and stepped out onto the walkway, patting the pocket of his shorts to make sure he had his key, and then closed the door behind him. It was time to shove internal philosophical debates aside and speak to somebody who could give him real information, whether she wanted to or not.

Lance turned right and started for the office.

He did not get far.

Standing on the walkway, Lance turned and stared at his motel room's window. He was completely certain that the blinds had been down and the curtains drawn when he'd left. But now, he was looking through the glass and directly into his room. The lights were off, but the television was on, another episode of *Full House* on the screen, the flickering glow of color bouncing soft light across the room. There was somebody asleep in the bed, a sweatshirt hood pulled up around their head, their entire body buried beneath the comforter, the shape rising and falling slowly with each breath the person took.

Lance was watching himself sleep. Of course he'd recognized the hoodie at once, and though it was a mind-bending experience to witness a living version of yourself that was, well, not yourself at that given moment, who better to know the size and shape and layout of your own body than you?

Lance had no doubt he was viewing himself through the glass like some peepshow, but unlike before, when what he'd seen had all been events from the past, this scene was different. Lance had never been to this motel before. Not until tonight. And the only time he'd slept had been when he'd first arrived and had had the dream where he'd seen Quinten for the first and then witnessed himself right before he'd entered room six. He'd fallen asleep with the lights on that time, he was certain of that. So if what he was seeing wasn't something from the past, that meant it was possible that what he was seeing now was...

The future, he thought. *This hasn't happened yet.*

And just as he thought this, a person came into view from the right side of the window, appearing from the shadows like a child's monster from their closet. Slow, lurking with frightening purpose.

The knife was clutched in their right hand, its long blade glinting in the glow from the television, short bursts of light as the person moved across the room toward the bed. Lance watched as he remained motionless beneath the comforter, unaware of the new presence in the room with him.

Move, he wanted to yell. *Get away!*

The words built up in his throat but they did not escape. Lance swallowed them down, knew they'd do no good.

He could only stand and watch as the person raised the knife above their head and then brought it down with ferocity, sinking the blade into the comforter and the person beneath.

And then again.

Again and again and again and again. Each stab of the knife

causing Lance to flinch as he stood in the cold and helplessly watched himself be murdered.

Finally, the person with the knife stopped. Standing still over Lance's slaughtered body, waiting.

Then Lance noticed something different about the scene. Something subtle, but significant. Something that was, and then suddenly wasn't.

The shape beneath the comforter had stopped its methodical rise and fall. Lance in the bed was no longer breathing.

The person with the knife turned around then, moving to head toward the door, and in the light of the television screen, Lance looked into Meriam's face and saw the tears running down her cheeks.

26

LANCE PUSHED THROUGH THE MOTEL'S OFFICE DOOR, THE bell announcing his entry. Meriam was standing behind the check-in counter, her arms crossed and her eyes serious. No hint of the polite hospitality from earlier, yet not quite aggressive either. Lance shook the bits of snow from himself and then pulled down his hood. He stared back at Meriam. Now that he was here, and after what he'd witnessed in his motel room's window, he was quickly trying to figure out how to play this. Ultimately, he landed on an option that was dangerous. But given his current situation, he was okay with playing the high risk–high reward game.

He would be completely honest.

"Come on back," Meriam said and turned and disappeared into the back living space. Lance followed her, feeling as though he were passing through so many memories as he crossed the floor and rounded the counter, the visions of all he'd witnessed happening years ago replaying in his head like a quick recap to reinforce his reason for being here.

The coffeepot was on a pot holder atop the small table, two mugs steaming from their brim set at either seat. Meriam was already seated, waiting. Her eyes locked onto Lance as he entered and never let him go. Lance sat across from her, lifted his mug to his lips and took a sip. Too hot, again, but so good. Time travel had made him thirsty. He took another long sip, gulping down a third of the mug, and as he drank, he looked over the bottom of the mug and beyond Meriam, over her shoulder to the kitchen counter where, sitting right next to the toaster, was a butcher block full of knives.

He gently set the mug back down. Meriam waited, clearly intent to let him make the first move. Lance understood; she'd kept secrets for so long, she wasn't going to give them up now without a compelling reason.

Lance took one more sip of coffee and then cleared his throat. "You have a nephew," he said. "His name is Quinten. He's tall like me, and slim like me. When I first arrived tonight, you thought I was him. Understandable. Because from the back, and from a distance, we look the same. It's only when you can see our faces clearly that you can tell the difference. That's why you asked me what you did when you first saw me. You said, 'Is it you? Is it *really* you?'"

Meriam opened her mouth to speak, but Lance cut her off. He was just getting started. "But our looks aren't the only way your nephew and I are similar. He has special abilities, special talents. I don't know for sure how much of them he shared with you, but I'm talking about things like being able to find lost items with ease, knowing information about people or places that nobody else could possibly know, with no satisfactory explanation as to how. And bigger things, perhaps"—*here comes the honesty*—"like being able to get inside people's heads, hear their thoughts. And not just the living, either. I believe your nephew might have the ability to see and hear spirits. Communicate with the dead, if you will."

At this, Meriam's eyes grew larger, and again she tried to

214

interject. But again, Lance cut her off, holding up a hand to silence her.

"There's two reasons I both know and, more importantly, *believe* these things about your nephew. The first is because I'm the same way. That's why I say we're similar. All those things I just mentioned that your nephew is able to do, I can do them as well. For the longest time, I've thought I was completely alone in this. I've always wondered if there were others, and had honestly assumed that there must be, somewhere out there. I refused to believe that in the entire world, I was the only one. But I'd never come across anyone else. Not even close." Lance paused, catching his breath.

"The second reason I know and believe these things about your nephew is because I've seen it. I've seen *him* and some of the things he's done. I've heard conversations between him and you and your late husband, Murry. This might sound crazy to you, but I'm willing to bet it won't, because you've spent a good portion of your life with somebody like Quinten, who has probably told you stories like the one I'm telling now, and you know that no matter how ridiculous, how much like science fiction or a ghost story it might sound, you know it's true. Because you've seen behind the curtain, so to speak. You've seen too much of the evidence to deny it or pretend to discourage it.

"When I called you back and said I'd gotten held up, what I really meant was I somehow got lost, found myself *living* in the past of this motel. I walked room to room to room, walked in this office. I relived very specific moments of yours and Murry's and Quinten's lives that I feel must be important, if maybe for no other reason than to let me know that I'm not alone."

Meriam sat and stared silently. Like she'd suddenly fallen into a state of shock.

But Lance wasn't finished. He couldn't stop, wouldn't rest

until he'd poured everything out, drained himself until he was empty and Meriam would have no possible angle for denial.

"If you want more proof, how about this: the letter. I know the woman who hanged herself in room one left you that letter, which I'm betting nobody but you has ever laid eyes on. I know about the Backstroms, too. How Murry murdered them and then covered it up. I'm guessing whatever he did worked pretty well, because he did it again, didn't he? With the man who died in room five, the cop with the young girl? Murry and Quinten made him disappear, too. I don't know why, I'll admit that, but I do know that it happened. I know Murry and Quinten got in an argument after the cop. Because getting rid of the cop had been Quinten's idea, but he hadn't known about the Backstroms, and that upset him.

"And I know about what happened in room six, too. I know why you say that room is off-limits. It's because something terrible happened there, and I'm guessing you just can't bring yourself to step foot inside it ever again."

Lance stopped there. Picked up his mug and drained his coffee. Refilled it from the pot on the table and then said, "Start talking. Please. I don't care about anything but answers, and where I can find Quinten. I think you'll agree he and I would be happy to see each other."

Meriam was quiet for a long time. Lance waited patiently, understanding that the bomb of knowledge he'd just dropped was certainly a lot to process for somebody who had likely spent most of their life keeping all this information locked away in their head, never whispering a word about any of it to another human being. Then Meriam raised her own mug to her lips, taking a small sip, and when she looked across the top of the mug at Lance, he saw the wet of tears in her eyes. She set the mug down, as gently as if it were made of the most delicate china, and asked, "You ... you actually saw him? You saw Quinten?"

Lance felt the heartbreak in the woman's voice. Whatever had happened between them all, it had clearly never been resolved. "Yes," he said, "but not now. Not in the present. Like I said, I saw things that happened here *before*. It was like I was living in a movie of your past."

Meriam, as Lance had assumed she would, did not try to rebuke this. "We loved him so much. He was like our own son."

Lance nodded. "Tell me about him."

She did.

Quinten was Meriam's sister's son. His father was a security guard at the rubber factory where his mother had worked, but he'd gotten fired and skipped town before Quinten was ever born.

Something else we have in common, Lance thought.

With not much money, an ever-changing shift schedule at the factory, and no father figure to help share the child-caring workload, Quinten's mother turned to her only sister and her husband for help.

"We were young, Murry and I, and had never really thought that we wanted kids of our own. Murry's father had bought the land and this motel—which was nothing but the bones at the time, having been shut down and abandoned long before—and had aspirations of fixing it up and running it with his son. But then Murry's pop died and we inherited it. Murry wanted to keep his father's dream alive, and I was fine with that. I had no real aspirations of my own, no real skills, and business owner sounded just fine to me. We didn't have time for Quinten, not really. We both had our jobs, and the motel took up most of our spare money and time, but as soon as I saw his little face in the hospital when Marsha delivered him, I fell in love. I think

Murry did, too. Right that very day. But he never would admit that to me."

Meriam smiled at the thought. Lance could see her drifting away, off to revisit those memories. She continued. "So, we became Marsha's full-time babysitters. Not only because we had more flexibility with our time, and there was two of us, but because, well ... my sister wasn't very motherly, if I'm being honest. Don't get me wrong, I do believe she loved her son, but she had a hard time expressing that love. She didn't know what to do with him when they were alone together, was constantly fretting about every little thing and how she was worthless and did it all wrong and that Quinten deserved somebody better than her. It got scary a couple times, the way she talked, like maybe she thought it would be better if either she or Quinten weren't around anymore. So, Murry and I took Quinten more and more, and things worked out okay for a while. Until the accident."

Marsha had been working her usual line job at the rubber factory and, while taking her scheduled fifteen-minute break, had rounded the corner of a storage aisle at the exact same time a forklift was coming around the same corner in the opposite direction. The forklift driver, failing to follow proper safety protocol, whether a habit or a simple one-time slipup, had failed to sound the forklift's horn in advance to alert foot traffic of its arrival.

Marsha spent a week in the hospital with neck and back injuries and left with an enormous check from the factory's parent company. A large payoff, to keep her from taking further legal action. To somebody in Marsha's position, it was a goldmine.

"But, she gave us the money," Meriam said. "Said to use it for the motel, and that she didn't need it." Meriam sighed. "We knew she was trying to repay us for essentially raising her son over the last few years, which was sweet, but also showed maybe how much she simply didn't understand parenthood. Anyway, we took the money, making sure she kept enough to be able to buy her townhouse she'd been renting and pay her bills and not have to work for a while. We were able to get the motel up and running, just the way Murry and his pop had always wanted. Quinten was starting elementary school and doing well. Things seemed okay."

But Marsha had become addicted to the pain pills she'd been prescribed after her injury.

"She had a history with drugs," Meriam said. "Marijuana, particularly. And she'd been smoking since we were barely teens, but those pills gripped her hard, and when the doctors refused to prescribe them anymore, she went to other sources, which led to other drugs, which led to my sister becoming a junkie who didn't know her own son's name some days.

"Quinten lived with us here until he got old enough to understand the situation fully, and big enough to take care of himself. Then he moved back home with Marsha. Because you see, he loved her. Just like she loved him. Even if both of them only did so out of instinct. Mother and son. Son and mother. It's just natural, I guess. Plus, Quinten's heart was bigger than his brain sometimes." Meriam looked at Lance hard then. "Which," she said, "I guess you already know, if you've really seen the things you've claimed to."

Lance nodded. "When did you know Quinten was special? When did you first realize he had different abilities?"

"Right away," Meriam said. "It was obvious right away to Murry and me. Would have been to anybody who spent that much time with him. When he was too young to understand how to hide what he could do, you know? Before he had to be discreet about it all."

Lance had to wonder how things would have been different

for Quinten if his mother had been the one to raise him, if she would have noticed, and what that might have meant. How that might have changed things. It seemed important, *vital*, maybe, that Meriam and Murry had taken Quinten in, and Lance had to wonder how much of an influence the Universe had played in that. Did the forklift driver often forget to sound the horn?

At this point, Lance knew he had more questions about what he'd seen from the motel's past, but his eagerness to learn more about Quinten, to get what he'd come for in the first place, was overwhelming.

"Where is he now?" Lance asked. "I really need to talk to him."

Meriam was quiet then. She stared at Lance for a long time, and something like uncertainty crossed her face for the first time since they'd started talking.

"You saw what happened in room six?" she asked.

Lance nodded. "I did." He kept his own role in what had happened in room six out of it for now, not wanting to have to take the time to explain. Didn't see how it would do much good.

"Then you should know where Quinten is," Meriam said. "He's dead."

[27]

A PART OF LANCE HAD ALREADY KNOWN THE BOY WAS dead.

It was a small, nagging itch at the back of his skull, but he'd done his best to ignore it, to silence its pestering. He'd fought off its advances into his consciousness so hard that he'd convinced himself otherwise. The boy had to be alive. They had to speak with each other. If not, what was any of this even about?

But there was something else. Burying down frustration, Lance asked, "If he's dead, why did you say what you did when I arrived tonight? Why did you think I might be him?"

Meriam closed her eyes and shook her head, a look that said she couldn't believe what she was about to say. "After everything else he could do, all the things that made him so special, I guess part of me—the part of me that wants so badly to be able to see him again—wouldn't have found it too crazy to think he could somehow have found a way to beat death."

Lance said nothing.

"And there was something about you," Meriam said. "I felt it, before you'd even come through the office door. It was like an anxiousness had started to grow in my belly. Alerting me, preparing me for your arrival. But it was a *good* feeling. It bordered on excitement." She paused. "I hadn't felt that since Quinten was here."

Lance searched for something to say. Wanted to ask more about this feeling, this sense that Meriam possessed that had alerted her to his arrival. Did others feel this way when he passed by, or were only those who were connected to people like he and Quinten tuned into the correct frequency?

"You really didn't know?" Meriam asked, breaking the silence that had grown long between them.

Lance looked at her, shook his head. "I ..." *I thought I'd saved him*, was what he was going to say. "I'm sorry."

Meriam offered a small smile and nodded. "It was the noise that woke us, something like an explosion," she said. "Murry and I had both jumped out of bed, middle of the night. We thought it must have been the storm. A tree branch blown down, or a fallen power line. When we went out to investigate, we saw room six's windows shattered and the door wide open and tire tracks in the snow. And..."—she took a breath to control her emotions—"that's when we found him. Taped to that chair. The room a mess. Like a bomb had gone off."

Me, Lance thought. *I did that.*

"That image of him, his eyes open and his head hanging limp, his beautiful face twisted in pain ... that's the image that haunts me at night. It's why I can't sleep. When we found him that night, it was the first time we'd seen him in months. Ever since he and Murry had their argument the night they..."

She paused and looked at Lance.

"It's okay," he said. "The night they got rid of the cop's body. I told you, I already know. That's not what I care about. I'm not here to get you in any sort of trouble. After all, how long has it been?"

"Over twenty years," Meriam said. "But I still see him clear as if it were yesterday."

Over twenty years ... I was barely born.

Meriam wiped her eyes and kept going. Like Lance had felt before, it was as though, now that she'd started, she was ready to let it all out, a great expulsion of secrets that had been choking her for over two decades.

"The county coroner said it was heart failure, but they'd also found signs of a stroke. A hemorrhaging in the brain. They couldn't give us a cause, but it was assumed he'd been under great distress during whatever had happened in that room. We never found out what, of course. There were no marks of physical harm on his body, aside from the tape that had been applied. Police were no help. Said it looked like a robbery, even though nothing had been stolen. Vandals, maybe, and Quinten had tried to stop them and they'd decided to have some fun with him. I knew it was all bullshit, but what could we do? Other than ... other than feel guilty."

Lance shook his head. "There's nothing you could have done. You might have ended up dead, too. You and Murry both. Trust me."

Meriam closed her eyes, squeezing out a fresh wave of tears. "Trust me," she said. "That's what Quinten always used to say to me. Every time I got worried or anxious about something he was up to, every time I acted like I knew what was best for him, he would always give me that look, that sly smile of his, and say, 'Trust me.'"

She shook her head. "I should have. Who am I, honestly? Why would somebody like me, so unremarkable, so *average*, think I knew what was best for somebody like him? Somebody who possessed knowledge and understanding that made my head dizzy with incomprehension. What did I know about *anything*? Nothing, that's what. And I killed him."

"It's not your fault," Lance offered. *I couldn't save him either.*

"But it is!" Meriam hissed, her eyes coming alive with pain. "I didn't trust him." Then she lowered her head and closed her eyes again and shook her head, as if to clear it. When she looked back to Lance, he saw guilt in her eyes. "It's my fault that nice young couple died. The Backstroms. It's my fault Murry shot them."

Lance remembered the conversation he'd overheard, looking through the door into Meriam and Murry's living space—an argument from the past. "You were worried about something," he said. "Something the Backstroms did made you uneasy. You were scared for Quinten. Why?"

Meriam laughed, a sarcastic, dismissive sound. "You're going to think I'm terrible when you hear it."

Lance shook his head. "I told you, I'm not here to judge. I just want to know what happened. I've seen most of this story, but I need you to fill in the gaps."

Meriam sighed. "It's simple and stupid. No other way to put it. It was just past sundown, the day that the Backstroms had met with Quinten, and I walked over to their room to see if they needed anything before Murry and I turned in for the night. I got to their door and was about to knock when I heard them talking inside. The man was getting very loud—not angry, but excited. He seemed very happy, and he kept telling his wife over and over, 'The boy's a God-honest medium. Has to be!' And he started talking about how Quinten could have his own television show or big events out in Vegas. The man kept saying he didn't understand why Quinten lived *here* when he could be rich, have anything he wanted."

And you panicked, Lance thought, understanding now. *You thought they would expose him, when exposure was the last thing he wanted.*

"I got scared, you see?" Meriam said. "I didn't know where exactly the Backstroms were from, or what they did for a living. Didn't know what sort of connections they might have. I even disconnected the phone line for their room because I was worried that I was only one phone call away from having Quinten's life turned completely upside down.

"When Murry got home from fishing with his buds, I was in a complete panic. And I was *angry*. I wasn't going to sleep unless I knew Murry and I did everything we could to keep the Backstroms from destroying our lives—because that's what it would have been, if they'd ruined Quinten. It would have ruined us all."

Lance said nothing. Only nodded.

"So I came up with the idea to scare them. But *that's all*, you see? I didn't want anybody to get hurt. I wasn't a murderer. But I would do anything to keep Quinten's secrets safe. To keep *our* secrets safe. Murry was against the whole thing, of course, but I knew he'd go along with it. He would do anything for me, just like I'd do anything for Quinten."

Lance remembered the way that the dead man's body had been splayed out, half on the bed and half off, like he'd fallen forward off the front and onto the floor. "But you weren't expecting them to fight back," Lance said. "That's what happened, right? The man tried to defend them and Murry shot him."

"*Accidentally* shot him! He swore he had the safety on, but ... apparently not. He reacted, that's all. Same as anyone would. Mr. Backstrom lunged for him and Murry got spooked and shot him."

"And the woman?" Lance asked. "Why her?"

Meriam looked away then, something in her demeanor hardening. She was quiet for a few seconds, as if searching for the right way to explain. But Lance already knew the explanation. It was the only thing that fit. He said, "You couldn't have any witnesses. Murry had already killed the man. How could he possibly leave the woman alive without ending up in jail? Is that it?"

Meriam looked back to him again, her eyes defiant, ready to defend her husband's actions. "What would you have done?"

Lance shook his head. "I don't know, ma'am. Honestly."

"Sure you do," Meriam said. Lance could see the anger rising in her. As if, now that she'd admitted what had happened, she was second-guessing her decision. Lance was all at once aware at how, after all these years, the woman before him still had not fully processed the events from her past. "This is the part where you're going to tell me there were other ways we could have resolved things, or that we should have told Quinten, or ... or ..." She slammed her fists onto the table, spilling coffee from over the brim of her and Lance's mugs. "How could you possibly understand what we were dealing with?"

Lance gave her a minute, letting some of the adrenaline fade from her veins. Then, softly, he said, "My mother killed herself to keep me alive."

Meriam's face blanked. She sat back in her chair as if she'd been shoved.

"The same people who killed Quinten, the ones who had him in room six, they came after me, too. They would have caught me then, if my mother hadn't done what she did. She ended her life, and I ran. This was only a few months ago, so I'm still hyperaware of what people are willing to do to protect the ones they love."

The refrigerator hummed and the coffeemaker gave off a gurgle from the counter. Lance stood from the table, grabbed a paper towel from the roll by the sink and came back to wipe up the spilled coffee. Tossed the wet towels in the trash and then sat back down.

Meriam had calmed down. She looked at Lance now with sympathy, and also something else. Something that might have said, *We're really on the same side, aren't we?*

"I know what you want to ask," Lance said. "So go ahead."

"Who are they? Who are the people that killed Quinten?" Meriam's voice carried a thirst for vengeance.

Lance shook his head. "Nobody you're ever going to have to worry about again. I don't know many specifics myself, but as far as I can tell, they're hunters. They hunt people like me and Quinten, people with our gifts. These two hunters, they have gifts of their own, too. But different. In its simplest form, it's a battle of Good and Evil. Quinten and I are the Good."

Meriam nodded her head, as if this all made perfect sense. But then it looked like she was considering something, contemplating a new piece of evidence. "Who sent them? What do they want with you all?"

Lance shook his head. "I've told you all I know."

Which wasn't exactly true. For instance, Lance knew that the reason the Reverend and the Surfer went after Quinten seemed to be different than the reason they'd come after him in Hillston. The Reverend had made it clear to Lance in their conversations that they'd wanted Lance to join them, to use his powers for their side. That together they would become extremely powerful.

At least that was the sales pitch. The ruse.

But with Quinten, they'd been digging. They'd abused his mind, searching. They'd wanted information only. Something the boy had locked away in his thoughts. What that thing was, Lance didn't know.

"You know," Meriam said, "sometimes I got the feeling Quinten knew something like that was going to happen. Maybe I'm only trying to convince myself in retrospect, but I swear ...

sometimes, the way he talked—it was like he knew his time was limited. Do you think that could be true?"

Lance remembered the look he'd seen on Quinten's face as he'd told his aunt to trust him that day in the motel's office. "I think it's possible, yes," Lance said. "Your nephew had many gifts. I wouldn't doubt he could have sensed something bad might have been on its way."

Meriam shook her head. "And he never said a word to us about it." She smiled. "Either too brave or too stubborn, or both."

Lance said nothing.

"After all these years," Meriam said, "I may not understand it all, but at least I won't die completely in the dark as to what happened that day. So, for that I want to say thank you. I'm sorry if I became rude. It's just ... well, I didn't want you to—"

"It's fine," Lance said. "You're perfectly fine. Your nephew seemed like a fine boy, and I'm very sad I won't get to meet him."

Meriam looked as though she were going to say something and then stopped. Instead, she pushed her chair away from the table and walked to the bedroom, disappearing out of sight, replaced with the sounds of a drawer opening and some things being shoved aside. She returned a moment later with something small and white in her hand. "Here," she said, handing the thing to Lance. "You can have it."

Lance took the object from her—a folded white piece of paper, yellowed with age. Meriam's name scribbled across the front. The letter from the dead woman in room one.

"She was very nice," Meriam said. "We chatted a bit when she first arrived. She seemed very sad, and I was trying to be friendly and cheer her up. I don't know why she addressed the letter to me instead of Quinten. I assume it's because she thought it would be me or Murry that would find her." Meriam shrugged. "Anyway, I used to read it whenever I wanted to remember how pure Quinten was. How much good there was in him." And then, like a switch being flipped, Meriam's eyes filled with tears again and she spoke through a sob, saying, "I never even showed it to him. I was so selfish. I thought ... I ... I didn't want him to feel responsible for her, for that woman killing herself. I know he did, still. Probably would have either way. She thought the letter would make it better, but I thought it would have only rubbed salt on the wound. Yet there I was, all these years reading the letter for my own comfort. What a terrible person I am." She wiped the tears from her cheeks and said, "God, all I ever tried to do was protect him, and look where it got me. In the end, none of it mattered. He's still dead. And I'm alone with nothing but time to think about it."

Lance stood and slid the letter into his pocket, sensing it was time for him to leave. He could offer Meriam nothing more to set her mind at ease, and he felt there wasn't anything else she could tell him that would be useful.

"Thank you," he said. "For the talk and for the coffee. I'm sorry we had to meet this way, but I want you to know I do appreciate what you've been able to tell me, and I'm truly sorry about Quinten. I don't know what lies beyond, but I hope you get to see him again someday."

Lance turned to leave, but as he reached the door to head back into the office area, Meriam called out, "You ... you aren't going to turn me in, are you? About Murry killing those people, about us hiding it all these years?"

Lance gave her a sad smile. "Trust me," he said.

And then he slid out the door into the office, quickly and quietly grabbing the one thing he needed before he made his way outside, back into the snow.

THE WIND HAD DIED DOWN TO BARELY A BREEZE, NOT EVEN enough to cause a rustle from the trees. The snowfall had reduced itself to scattered flakes, drifting down solo, like stragglers trying to catch up with the rest of the pack. The clouds were rolling out, revealing the sky above. The moon was fading away, a dimmed spotlight on the parking lot. Soon it would be morning, the sun cresting the horizon and burning open a start to a new day. But for now, everything was still and quiet and calm.

Meriam crept from the office the few short steps to room one's door. She stopped, startled to find that the window blinds were up and the curtains open, allowing her to look right in. Her first instinct was to drop down, quick, and hopefully unseen. But it was too late. She'd already come this far; anything other than acting completely normal would be suspicious. So, she stood, braved a look in through the window, and then let out a sigh of relief.

The room was dark except for the flicking light of the television, which was showing an old sitcom that had gone off the air. She couldn't remember the name, but she knew it was about a big family living in one big house. The American Dream, some might say. But not hers, not Murry's either. They'd liked being just the two of them, way out here with nobody to bother them, running their own business, being their own bosses. And they'd had Quinten, their nephew who was really more like their son. The three of them had been all the family they needed. It had been perfect, in a lot of ways. Not always easy, but perfect, still.

Until tragedy had reached its ugly and gnarled hand from the ground and snatched Quinten away from them.

But until that day, they'd all been so strong together. And while losing Quinten had temporarily weakened her and Murry's resolve, they'd eventually decided together that the two of them moping around, blaming themselves, blaming others, being consumed by Quinten's death, would be the exact opposite of what their nephew would have wanted. So they pushed on, tried to live a happy life together the way they had before. They talked of Quinten fondly and often, hoping that the pain would eventually subside and the memories would allow themselves to be brought forth without the veil of sorrow surrounding them.

After the police investigation had concluded—all too fast, in her and Murry's opinion—they'd repaired room six and then considered it open for business once more.

But Meriam never allowed it to be occupied again. She wasn't sure why. Best she could figure, it was just her own way of preserving a part of her nephew. It was almost as if room six had become hallowed ground in her eyes. She never went in herself, either. She'd made Murry go in to clean and change the sheets and everything else that went along with the rooms' upkeep, regardless of occupancy, but once he'd passed away, she'd kept the door locked and tried not to think about what might be growing behind it.

The worst part, though, the part that sometimes made her ill with guilt—even more so than when she'd decided to blame herself for Quinten's death—was the part of her that sometimes felt her life had actually gotten *easier* since they'd lost him. Because with Quinten no longer around, she suddenly found it much easier to keep his secrets. To keep all their secrets. The evidence—or rather, anybody who might be searching for it— had essentially died with Quinten.

Murry had done a good job of getting rid of the bodies and the vehicles. He'd lived in the area his whole life, hunting and fishing and hiking and exploring every inch of the forest and mountains. He'd known exactly where to go, and it must have been a good place, because as far as Meriam knew, neither the Backstroms nor the cop had ever been found.

She'd kept her secrets for so long. First to protect her nephew's memory, and then later to protect her husband's.

Meriam looked through the motel room's window at the bulky shape hidden beneath the comforter. She thought the guy was right, that he and Quinten really would have liked to meet each other, and it was tragic that their paths had never crossed. She wondered how many others like them there might be. Tried not to think about what impact there might be if there was soon going to be one less.

Because even though she'd willingly told the guy her story in a long-overdue moment of catharsis, a story that he'd already figured out on his own, her motel had been home to her family's secrets for a long, long time.

And she intended to keep it that way.

She gripped the knife tightly in one hand and with the other slid her master key gently into the lock on the door, glancing out the side of her eye as she did so, looking for any movement from the shape beneath the comforter. Once inside, she'd have to control her emotions, not let her adrenaline rush her, making her sloppy. She needed just a few good strikes, right in the chest and neck. That should do it. That should be enough to end him quick.

The door unlocked and she pushed inside, quietly closing the door behind her, not wanting the cold to rush inside and wake him.

She took a moment to let her eyes adjust, the light from the television helping to light her way. The volume on the set was turned way down, and suddenly her own breathing sounded very loud. She closed her eyes, counted slowly to ten, inhaling and exhaling with each count.

I have to do this, she thought. *For Quinten. For Murry. For us.*

And then she was moving across the room, as if on air. Floating. She was in front of the bed, looking down at the shape beneath the comforter. He'd pulled the blanket completely up and over his head, like a child who was hiding from the monsters.

"I'm so sorry," she whispered to the room, feeling emotions overrun her, the warmth of tears on her cheeks.

She raised the knife high, feeling herself transition from accomplice to murderer, and then brought it down, throwing all her weight into it, wanting to bury the blade deep, wanting to make sure she got the job done.

Turned out, it was a wasted effort. Because the blade met almost no resistance at all, slicing through the shape beneath the comforter before plunging into the mattress, all the way to the hilt.

Lance had been standing watch for the last couple hours, waiting by the window, sneaking glances out from behind the curtain and fighting off sleep. As soon as he saw Meriam make her way inside room one and heard the door close behind her, he slid out the door of room two as quietly as he could, leaving the key he'd swiped from the office earlier on the bedside table.

He pulled his hood up over his head, adjusted the straps of his backpack, and headed off across the parking lot, not bothering to stick around and watch through the window as Meriam attempted to murder a stack of pillows.

He'd been counting on the fact that she'd be too worked up to notice that the shape beneath the comforter wasn't exactly proper human proportions, and also wasn't breathing. But even if Lance had been wrong, and she'd quickly realized his attempt at trickery, he wasn't worried. He didn't think she'd chase him. She was acting in desperation, he figured. An uncertainty about her past, and fear that she'd revealed too much to him driving her into a temporary moment of irrational behavior. She'd would settle down, and Lance would be long gone.

The only reason Lance had allowed himself to stay put at the motel was to see if the vision that he'd seen through his room's window would come true. If the Universe, after thrusting him into the past, was actually allowing him to see the future. Turned out it had all been accurate. A warning, that was what he'd decided. Play time was over, time to move along.

Trust me, he'd said to Meriam.

But she hadn't.

He didn't blame her, not exactly. She'd never fully understood her nephew, so Lance couldn't expect her to fully understand him, either. And who was he to her, anyway? Just a stranger calling in the night.

She needn't worry, though. She'd spent her life keeping her secrets in order to protect Quinten, and Quinten had done the same for her and Murry. Quinten's decision was good enough for Lance. He would respect it. It would be Lance's own way of honoring the boy he'd never met.

Lance, more than most, understood the sacrifices people make for family.

He reached the edge of the parking lot, his sneakers not quite touching the edge of the road. Here was where he'd entered, the place where he'd crossed over earlier. Here was the barrier where, in the past, he was not allowed to pass through.

But I'm done now, he thought. *It's finished. I learned what I needed to, and that's enough for now. I learned that I might not be alone in this after all.*

He stepped into the road. Felt the snow crunch beneath his feet.

He was free.

He turned and started walking along the snow-covered asphalt, letting the moon light his way. He did not look back. He'd seen enough of what was behind him. It was time to look forward.

[29]

Lance had walked a mile, and then two things happened. First, the trees began to thin out, replaced with fields and the occasional house or farm nestled off the road, long gravel driveways snaking toward them. Some had lights on inside, others were dark. The early risers versus those who preferred to wait for the sun. Second, the snow stopped.

Completely.

It wasn't simply that the accumulation had seemed less here than what lay behind Lance. No, it was as if a line had been drawn across the earth. On one side, the road was slick with slush and snow, Lance's sneakers wet and heavy. On the other side, the ground was dry, the asphalt a dusty gray instead of the wet black you'd expect, the grass dead and stiff instead of soggy and bent, weeping with melted snow. Lance looked to his left, where two farmhouses sat separated by maybe two acres of land between them. One yard had snow, the other did not. He wondered what the morning conversations might be between the two residents if they met at the end of their driveway to collect their morning papers. *Well, George, I told you that was the wrong type of seed for this climate. Guess you should have listened, huh?*

Lance would have bet money that if he'd turned around and walked the mile back to the motel and then kept going, he'd have come across another such demarcation. He didn't know how large of a circumference this snowy barrier consisted of, but he understood its purpose.

It was to slow me down and keep me put. The motel was the only place I was supposed to end up.

He couldn't help but think there'd been some sort of symbolism between the fact that it had been snowing fiercely when he'd arrived at the motel—*an unexpected storm, not even forecast by the weather folk*—just like it had been the night Quinten had been killed by the Reverend and the Surfer.

But maybe he was just tired. Tired and hungry.

Just as the sun began to rise, and the temperatures along with it, Lance heard the sound of a car coming up behind him. He stepped off the road and squinted against the morning light peeking over the trees. A boat of a car, an old Oldsmobile or something like it, long and low and loud, was maybe a quarter mile away. Its lights were on, weak against the rising sun, but strong enough to keep Lance from looking at the car head-on. He was exhausted, and even though he figured the town to be close, he wasn't going to turn down the chance of a ride. He'd had luck with Neil and the box truck. Maybe his luck would continue.

It didn't.

As the car grew closer, Lance stuck out his thumb, causing the vehicle to slow to nearly a stop, still about fifty yards away, before it suddenly burst to life, the engine grumbling and whining as the accelerator was smashed and the tires did a quick skip on the asphalt before finding purchase. The car flew past Lance, fast enough to cause him to take two quick steps further back off the road. And then it was nothing but taillights growing faint in the distance.

He hadn't even gotten a look at the driver.

Disappointed, but not deterred, Lance summoned what strength he had left and kept walking.

Soon, around another bend, the tops of the town's taller buildings came into view. A clock tower, presumably a courthouse, signaled civilization.

At a crossroads, he made a right. Then a left.

Then he saw the diner.

He was seated at a booth in the rear, right next to the alcove that housed the restrooms. It was wonderfully warm inside the diner, and the air was alive with coffee and eggs and bacon and everything life should smell like. He ordered everything, ate it all like he didn't know when he'd eat again. Washed it down with an entire pot of coffee, which he'd politely asked the waitress to leave at the table. She'd winked at him and said, "Long night, Hun?"

"Yes, ma'am," Lance had said. "Felt like it lasted years."

She laughed and touched his shoulder and said, "I know the feeling, babe." Then she'd sauntered off to her other tables, leaving Lance with his coffee and his thoughts.

And he thought for a long time, about everything. He replayed the events he'd seen at the motel, listened again to Meriam's story in his mind. Shook his head at how similar his life and Quinten's were on so many levels. Marveled again, with a certain bit of elation, at how, for the first time in his entire life, he knew that somebody else like him had walked this Earth, lived the same way he'd been forced to live, carried the same burdens and used the same gifts.

And when Lance had had the chance to save him, he'd failed.

It was right there in the booth that Lance knew what he had

to do. Even though the coffee and food had helped to reinvigo-rate him, he was still craving sleep, wanting nothing more than to ask the waitress where the nearest place to rent a room might be—the nearest place not behind him, that was. But he wasn't finished. One last thing needed his attention.

So when the waitress came back with his check, he handed over his cash, including a handsome tip, and asked, "Could you tell me where the town cemetery is, please?"

Turned out, it was only three blocks away, behind the Methodist church.

Lance stepped outside and headed toward the sidewalk, just catching sight of a car speeding out of the diner's parking lot.

A beat-up silver Oldsmobile, long and low and disappearing around the corner, leaving a plume of exhaust in its wake.

Lance Brody did not believe in coincidences.

The Methodist church was old, peeling gray paint and a leaning banister on the steps leading up to the front entrance, but its spire stretched high and proud, the cross atop it staring back at the clock tower in the center of town like a young sibling waiting for its older brother to make the first move. The stained-glass windows were bright and free from grit and dirt as the sun, which had climbed higher into the sky, heliographed secret messages to Lance as he found the rutted road on the side of the building and followed it around to the rear.

He stopped.

The cemetery was vast, not a simple plot of land with several congested stones and markers, but sprawling acreage that stretched far beyond the church and butted against the dense forest that lay beyond. Sycamore trees lined the road that weaved its way in a well-plotted loop around the grounds, mostly dead now, but in the spring and fall, Lance bet it was a beautiful sight.

It was peaceful. Exactly the way the resting place of the dead should be.

He scanned the area and saw he was alone. Exactly as he'd prefer it.

He started walking.

He followed the road halfway around its loop, breathing in deep the smells of the grass and the dead leaves and the impending arrival of winter in the air. He let it all guide him, take his hand and lead him. Sometimes, Lance felt he could literally let his mind leap from a tall building, or lie on its back in the waters and float, trusting the Universe to take hold, steer him in the right direction, allow him to land softly and safe.

Just past an ancient sycamore with a U-shaped branch jutting from its trunk, Lance stepped off the road and made his way onto the grass, selecting a row of headstones and letting his fingers glide atop their surfaces as he passed, following the line until he reached the one that had been calling him.

He stopped, turned and looked down.

There was nothing special about the marker; gray stone, polished, but becoming rough with years of weather. Not unlike the others around it. Not worse, not better. Nothing to signify the type of person or type of life it represented. Lance read Quinten's name etched into the rock. And something about the sight of the boy's name caused a surge of emotion to land in Lance's throat. The empathy was overwhelming. The sadness, now that Lance was as close to face-to-face as he'd ever be with the boy—so close, yet so far away—was almost too much to bear. Lance fell to the ground, tossing his backpack aside and sitting on his butt and cradling his face into his hands, flushed with grief that gripped him and demanded he take notice.

"I'm so sorry," Lance said into his hands. "I tried. I tried to understand, I tried to help you. I ... I failed. I hope you can forgive me."

There was a beat of silence. A breeze blowing across the cemetery, grabbing Lance's message and carrying it away.

"Hi, Lance."

Lance's head lifted from his hands at the sound of the voice. Found Quinten sitting on his headstone, his long legs stretched out in front of him, crossed at the ankles.

"I've been waiting."

[30]

JUST LIKE THAT, THE REPEATED MESSAGE FROM THE MOTEL visions resounded in Lance's head. *He'll be waiting.* All this time, Lance had interpreted it as a warning, a threat that he'd forgotten since he'd left the motel's parking lot. It hadn't been a threat at all, but instead a wonderful promise.

The only thing that kept Lance from pushing himself off the ground and rushing toward Quinten, throwing the two of them together in an embrace, was the fact that Lance knew he was only seeing the boy's spirit. With so much happiness and an overwhelming sense of comradery thick in the air between them, Lance had never wanted to hug a person more in his life. Yet he could not. So he sat where he was, on the grass before the boy's tombstone, and stared in awe, searching for the right words, wondering where the two of them should even start their conversation.

Quinten started for him. "You can see me, right? Like, actually *see* me?"

Lance squinted in confusion. "Yes. I can see you."

Quinten laughed. "Awesome. I never could. See them, I mean. Not completely."

Lance stared back. Said nothing.

Quinten laughed again. "I could hear them—the spirits, the dead—I could hear their voices, their thoughts, I guess. And I could feel them, their presence in a room, around me, like an energy. Sometimes I could see things, like a blurred vision, like heatwaves in the summer coming off asphalt. Movement when there was nothing there. And they could hear me, too. We could communicate, easy as you and I are now. But"—he gave Lance a sly grin and a shrug of the shoulders—"I could never see them like they were just another person in the room. Almost tangible, you know? But you can. You can do it all, right?"

A part of Lance was almost dismayed to learn that after all the excitement of finding another person who was like him in the world, a person who shared his abilities and all the struggles that came along with them, there was already a dividing line between them. A difference that separated them.

"Yes," Lance said. "But how do you ... how do you know?"

Quinten shrugged again. "Same way people like us always end up knowing stuff, right?"

And only to Lance—*people like us*—would this answer make sense. And with that, Lance felt better. They might not be identical in their abilities, but for the first time in his life, Lance had just shared an understanding with somebody about a part of his life that had always lived alone. It was the most gratifying of feelings. The urge to hug Quinten rushed up at him again. He shoved it down and, understanding that the Universe would not have brought him here—to the motel, the town, the cemetery, to Quinten—without a purpose, asked, "Why am I here?"

Quinten's face grew somber, the sly grin fading. "Because I have a message for you. It's something you already know, I think. But if not, you need to. It's something I've known for over twenty years. Ever since you were born. It's why I'm like this"— he pointed to himself—"and you're like that."

Lance considered this, searched the boy's face for deeper meaning. "You mean ... dead and alive?"

Quinten nodded, and Lance felt a cold chill wash through him.

"But," Quinten said, looking up to the sky and closing his eyes, as if gauging some unseen factor, "we still have some time, and I have so many questions. I've waited a long time to talk to somebody like you—like *us*. Tell me about yourself. Was your childhood as weird as mine?"

Quinten flashed a bright smile, and Lance burst out laughing. The moment was almost dreamlike, as if at any moment the feeling of happiness would fade and Quinten would vanish and Lance would awaken in a dark room with nobody to share his secrets with. The secrets he'd held for so long.

So Lance started talking.

It was euphoric, their talk. Two boys sitting together in a cemetery, swapping tales of their lives, moments of danger, humorous anecdotes, and tragic sadness. Both of them sharing things on a previously undiscussed level of intimacy reserved specifically for each other. They stripped away their reservations they'd spent so long building up, baring it all. Both of their stories culminated with their run-ins with the Reverend and the Surfer. The difference was Lance's story had more to be added, while Quinten's had come to an end.

The sun shifted across the sky as they talked, the hours passing. Finally, when the conversation eventually came to a stop, Lance offered what he'd initially come to say. After sharing this great moment together, the words that followed weighed even heavier on his heart.

"I want you to know I'm sorry," Lance said. "Sorrier than you can ever know. I tried to save you that day, but I couldn't."

"I know," Quinten said, his face falling a bit. "But see, that's why you're here, that's what I have to tell you."

Lance waited.

Quinten, who during their talk had moved to sitting in the grass with his back leaning against his headstone, said, "You weren't supposed to save me. I was saving you."

"I ... I don't understand," Lance said.

So Quinten explained. About how he'd known his end was coming, that his purpose in life had shifted the moment Lance had been born. Lance was a force unlike any other, a power stronger than any seen before. The darkness recognized it at once, felt his emergence the same way Quinten had, and they wanted him. Would stop at nothing to get to him.

"So we had to protect you," Quinten said. "Me and anybody else out there, I guess. Anyone else like us. Because if they were still out there, the others, they would have felt it just the way I had. We knew you were special. You were the one who would have to save the world from the darkness."

Lance took this like a blow to the gut, a sucker punch of guilt. His thoughts whirled, dancing between disbelief and denial and fear. A tango of emotions.

Salvation, he thought. Shaking his head at the memory.

"In the room," Lance said, "you said, 'Salvation.' You were talking about me?"

Quinten nodded. "It's what I used to call you. As good a name as any, right?"

Lance thought about this. "I think I prefer Lance."

Quinten asked, "How did you do it, anyway? How were you even *there*?"

Lance shook his head. "Honestly, I have no idea. Just add it to my list of superpowers, I guess. One minute it was 2015, the next, I was walking around in the past." He'd meant this as a joke, but Quinten just looked at him in astonishment. So Lance filled him in on what had happened, everything at the motel.

Though he left out the part about Meriam trying to kill him. Lance suspected that Quinten, having passed on, might actually know more details than he was letting on, but was preferring to hear Lance's side of things.

When Lance was finished, Quinten shook his head and said, "Unreal. You really are the one."

Lance said nothing. A rush of wind came through, bending the treetops.

"And now...," Quinten said, his voice sounding suddenly nervous, "it's my turn to apologize to you."

Lance, again, was confused. "What? Why?"

Quinten looked Lance in the eyes, his face serious and stern. "I failed you. The day I died, I tried to fight it. I tried my best, but in the end, right before you arrived, they were able to get in. He was just so *strong*. He pulled down all my defenses, and he didn't get much, but ... I guess in the end he got enough."

"What are you talking about?" Lance said, his heart racing in his chest.

"They pulled out a name," Quinten said. "I didn't know what it meant, and I don't think they did either at the time, but eventually..."

"What name? I don't understand?"

"Pamela," Quinten said. "They got the name Pamela from my mind. Your mother."

Lance was stunned.

"I'm so, so sorry," Quinten said. "My best wasn't enough."

Lance was quiet for a long time, a flood of memories of his mother playing in his head. Including the night she'd died, when the Reverend and the Surfer had ended her life.

She'd saved him. She'd made the choice. A choice Lance might not ever fully understand, though Quinten's testimonial was shedding more light on that understanding.

Finally, Lance said, "It's not your fault. They would have found me eventually. And, hey, they're so dumb it took twenty-three years, even with the clue." Lance smiled.

Quinten looked back at Lance, first with apprehension, as if waiting for more, and then, when nothing came, with gratitude.

"Thank you," he said.

The sound of a car's engine and tires on crushed gravel jolted Lance to attention. He turned and looked over his shoulder and saw the beat-up Oldsmobile round the side of the church and start down the cemetery's path. It drove just past the entrance and then stopped, engine idling.

"You need to go," Quinten said. "It's time."

"What?" Lance asked, suddenly desperate for more time with the boy.

"What happened at the motel, that sort of thing requires a lot of energy, you know what I mean? Like the stars sending up a signal flare. It'll leave a trace, too. Like a burnt-out campfire. The darkness will sense it, and they'll come looking. They'll be on your trail. Like they already have been."

Lance had told Quinten about the showdown on Sugar Beach's shore, about how the Reverend and the Surfer had met their end. And even though Lance had suspected as much, Quinten's warning helped to reassure these suspicions. The war was not over. If not the Reverend and the Surfer, it would be somebody else, still hunting him.

Lance looked over his shoulder again, back toward the Oldsmobile that looked like a rusted hunk of garbage in the otherwise pristine grounds. "Who is it?" Lance asked.

"Somebody who you can trust. They'll get you out of town. Wherever you want to go."

Quinten had stood again, so Lance did the same, pushing off the ground and reaching for his backpack. Right then, his phone vibrated in his pocket, shooting a buzz of adrenaline though him. He reached a hand in to grab it, felt a folded piece of paper and then remembered. "Oh!" he said. "I have something for you. A letter."

He moved to pull it out, but Quinten stopped him by saying, "I know what it says. She already told me. You keep it. Read it sometime. It might help."

Lance opened his mouth to speak and then stopped. What could he say?

"Be well, friend," Quinten said. "I'm glad to have met you. Now go be what the world needs you to be. Go kick some ass." He smiled that sly grin of his again, and then he faded away.

Lance stared at Quinten's headstone for another full minute, having to will himself to look away, to turn around and leave this place. Though the time had been short, Lance would be forever grateful for it. It had, in fact, reinvigorated him, sparked to life an enthusiasm and energy that had begun to grow dormant after his months of tragedy and travel.

Go be what the world needs you to be.

Lance reached out and rested his hand atop the boy's headstone. "Thank you," he whispered. Then he turned and followed the path to the waiting Oldsmobile.

As he approached the car, the driver's side window was cranked down, revealing for the first time the driver. Lance stepped around the front of the car and stood by the opened window.

He was hit with a slap of recognition, though he couldn't quite place the woman's face. Pretty, but tired. Kind, but wary. Maybe late thirties. Through the window opening, she was appraising Lance the same way he was appraising her. All the while, he couldn't shake the fact that he knew her somehow.

And then, like flipping over a playing card, the reveal was

instant. The last time he'd seen this face, it had been much, much younger. But it was the same face, he was certain.

"Hi," the woman said. "I'm Alexa."

It was the young girl from room five.

"Sorry if I scared you," Alexa said after Lance had climbed into the passenger seat. Inside, the car smelled like sweat and grease. A vanilla-scented air freshener was fastened to one of the air vents, working hard but failing to fight off the odor. Lance's feet crushed down a pile of fast-food bags on the floorboard. He set his backpack in his lap, turned and looked at the woman.

"Before, on the road," she said. "And again, at the diner. You probably thought I was crazy. Hell," she laughed, "maybe I am."

Lance said nothing. Alexa did a three-point-turn in the cemetery, the Oldsmobile's suspension sounding like rusted hinges, and then she drove back to the street. "I saw him in a dream," Alexa said. "You know, *him*, from the motel. I think you know him too, right? You must, if you're here. Quinten."

Lance nodded silently, waiting.

"It was the first time I've seen him since he helped me. After all these years. It's hard to believe, really, that I'd never dreamed of him. That some part of my subconscious hadn't dragged him up from my memory by now, considering how much of an impact he'd had on my life. He set me free, you see? When I was a little girl, he saved me. He..."

She stopped. Looked at Lance with a sudden fascination, as if the joke had been on her the whole time. "Do I need to tell you all this?"

Quinten's words again: *Somebody you can trust.*

"Not really," Lance said. "I think I understand." Then, "You've been alone ever since? Ever since that day at the motel?"

Alexa was quiet then, as if her past had suddenly rushed up behind her like a stranger in a dark alley. Then she said, "Yes. But that's okay. I'm a survivor. Maybe I got that from my dad, which I hate to admit, but hey, it is what it is. I've been all over, you see? I've been to every state, seen every national park. I've lived my life free and clear. Hell, I've been thirteen different people since I was twelve years old, at least on paper. And, yeah, it's had its ups and downs, but I wouldn't change it. I think he saw that. Quinten, I mean. That day when it all happened..." She'd been talking fast, rapid-fire, but paused here, looked over at Lance like maybe she was about to second-guess her trust in him.

"It's okay," Lance said. "Go on."

Alexa considered this for just another brief moment, then shrugged. "I think he saw my future—my *other* future. I think he knew that if they'd reported my dad's death, if I'd gone back home, I would have just ended up in the system, you know? State care, foster homes, who knows what kind of hell that would have been? Passed around like a damn commodity, never knowing if the next person who pretended to be my new dad was going to beat me or touch me or starve me. Hell, you've seen the stories on the news. You know exactly what I'm talking about." She flicked on the left turn signal and headed out of town. "Anyway, I think Quinten saw all that for me, and he knew he had to save me. So he did."

Lance remembered the look on Quinten's face when he'd made contact with the girl in room five, the way it had suddenly flashed with sadness. The girl was probably right, about everything. But Lance didn't need to tell her that. She knew well enough herself.

"And the dream?" Lance asked.

"Oh, right. I saw you and him talking, right back there in the cemetery."

For a second, Lance's mind went crazy with the thought that Alexa had actually been able to see Quinten in the cemetery with him, but then he understood. "We were together in the dream?" he asked.

She nodded, brushed a few strands of graying hair from her face. "You two were talking, over by his grave—I knew it was his grave for some reason, even though I've never been back here since that morning—and I couldn't hear anything you were saying. But then he was next to me, too. Quinten, I mean. He was still over by the tombstone, talking with you, but then he was next to me at the same time. And he told me then, he told me to come here and to trust you and take you wherever you wanted to go."

Lance looked at her, studied her face while she drove, the sun coming through the windshield lighting her features in a golden warmth. "So you just did it?" Lance asked.

Alexa shrugged. "It was just a feeling, you know? Like you know something to be absolutely true? Instinct, I guess you could call it. It was the same feeling I had that day at the motel. When he first walked into the room, I knew I could trust him. I still can't explain it. But, hey, it is what it is. You know?"

Lance nodded. "I know."

More so than you'll ever understand.

"Anyway, that's why I didn't pick you up on the road, and why I followed you from the diner. Something told me I wasn't supposed to get you until you'd had some time here, at his grave. Was I right?"

"Yes," Lance said. "You were. Thank you."

Alexa nodded, looking proud of herself.

They'd left town and were headed down the rural highway when Lance's phone vibrated in his pocket again. He reached in to pull it out and slid both it and the letter he'd gotten from Meriam out together. He set the phone aside for the moment and remembered Quinten's words. *Read it sometime. It might help.*

Lance unfolded the sheet of paper and started to read.

Quinten,

Do not feel guilty. This is not your fault. You have helped me more than anyone else could have. The goodness in you is palpable. Like the warm sun through the windows on a cold winter morning. You shed light into my darkness when I needed it the most and the rest of the world had failed me. You gave me the answers I'd needed. How much more would I have suffered? How much longer would I have clutched hope to my chest in an effort to believe my boy was still alive? I don't have to fight that battle any longer. I know where he is now, thanks to you. And I mean that sincerely, Quinten. It's all thanks to you. I am off to join him now. Because, as maybe only mothers can truly understand, I'd rather be dead with my boy, than alive without him. Again, do not feel guilty, Quinten. This is not your fault. All we can do is strive to help each other, because why else are any of us here? But in the end, we can only save ourselves. I will be forever in your debt, even in my death. Be well, Quinten. Thank you again, and I'll be sure and tell my son all about the nice young man who brought me back to him. All my love.

Lance read the letter twice before folding the paper back in half and returning it to his pocket. One phrase in particular had burned into his mind.

But in the end, we can only save ourselves.

Free will, Lance thought. It did exist. Maybe not to the fullest extent that most liked to believe, but it was real, all the same. And this filled Lance with hope, a warm fire in his belly that burned bright and spread up to his heart.

Lance picked up his flip phone from the seat next to him and opened it. The vibrations from earlier had been text messages from Leah.

Helloooooo?

Okay, seriously. Are you okay?

Lance smiled. He looked to Alexa and asked, "Do you mind if I make a phone call?"

She looked back at him and winked. "Is it a girl?"

Lance laughed. "It is."

Alexa nodded. "Thought so." She waved her hand at him, telling him to get on with it. "Don't mind me."

Lance thanked her and pressed the speed dial number for Leah.

She answered on the first ring. "Where have you been? Do you realize I've called you, like, a billion times?"

"Sorry," Lance said, filled with joy at the sound of her voice. "I had a really long night."

Thanks so much for reading **DARK VACANCY**. I hope you enjoyed it. If you *did* enjoy it and have a few minutes to spare, I would greatly appreciate it if you could leave a review saying so. Reviews help authors more than you can imagine, and help readers like you find more great books to read. Win-win!

-Michael Robertson Jr

For all the latest info, including release dates, giveaways, and special events, you can visit the page below to sign up for the Michael Robertson, Jr. newsletter. (He promises to never spam you!)

http://mrobertsonjr.com/newsletter-sign-up

Follow On:

Facebook.com/mrobertsonjr

Twitter.com/mrobertsonjr

More from Michael Robertson Jr

LANCE BRODY SERIES

Dark Vacancy (Book 4)

Dark Shore (Book 3)

Dark Deception (Book 2.5 - Short Story)

Dark Son (Book 2)

Dark Game (Book 1)

Dark Beginnings (Book 0 - Prequel Novella)

OTHER NOVELS

Cedar Ridge

Transit

Rough Draft (A Kindle #1 Horror Bestseller!)

Regret*

*Writing as Dan Dawkins

26695879R00158

Printed in Great Britain
by Amazon